ASTERAL'S KEY

An Inner Realm Adventure

MORIAH JOST

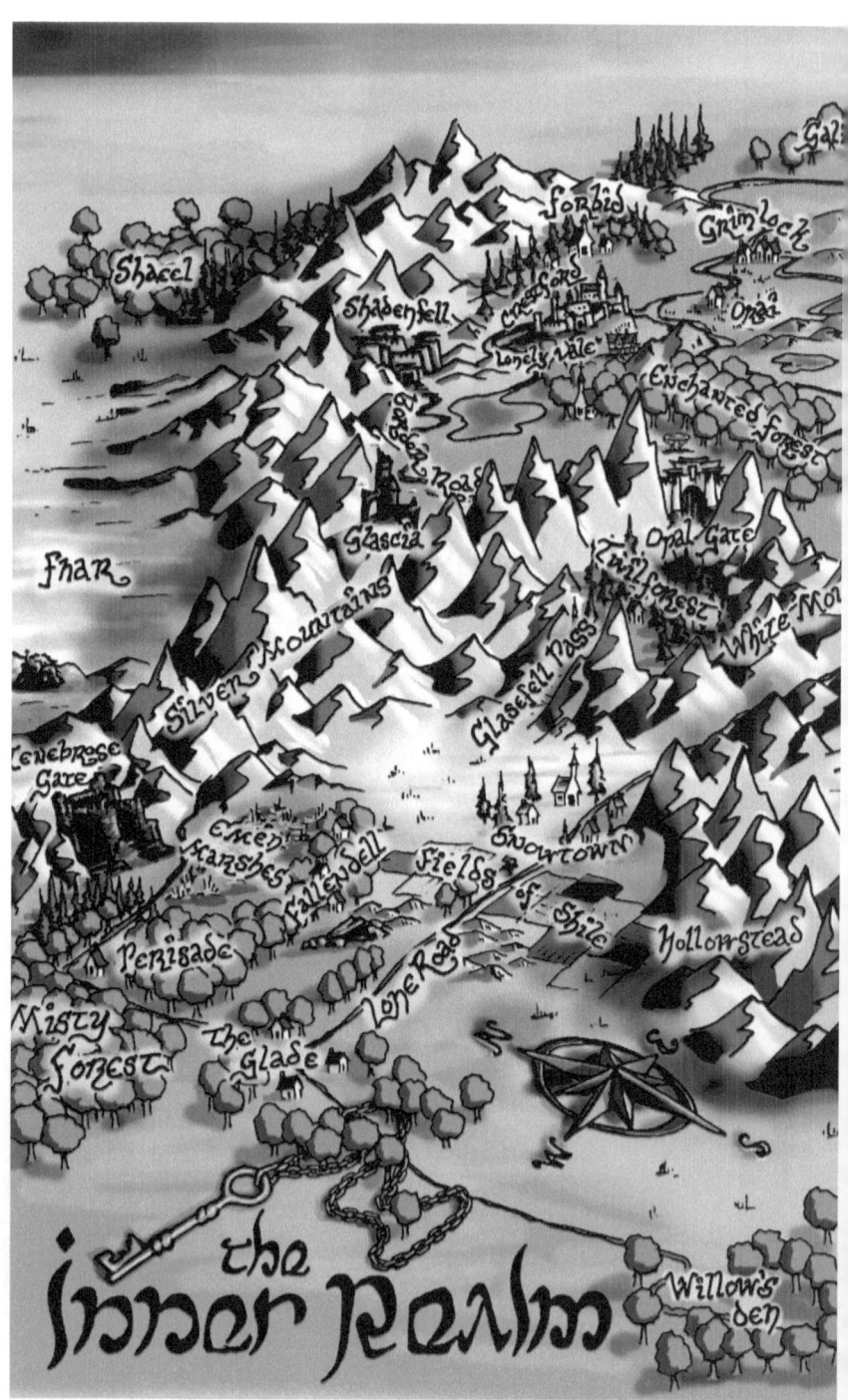

Asteral's Key
An Inner Realm Adventure

Dedication

*To the One who never
stopped believing in me.*

Endorsements

"Here is a young new author who creates a satisfying story that unfolds with every turn of the page. Throughout the book, Moriah is able to parallel fantasy with truth, leaving the reader to discover, like Selest, that the journey which lies ahead is a walk of faith with the One who leads."

—Kimberly Funk, children's book author

"While weaving together biblical truths and fast-paced elements, Asteral's Key hooked me immediately. As one who almost strictly reads nonfiction, the depth of content immediately drew me in. I thoroughly enjoyed the insight into a realm within which I typically would not be familiar. The plot, storyline, and characters were immediately enticing, and they successfully culminated in fulfillment."

—Debbie Oelke, Author of *Still Standing: Hope Beyond Disability*

"This story captures attention from the very first page. While there are religious elements tied in, this story will also very much appeal to the non-religious as well as the characters learn to look deep within themselves and depend on each other to find the strength to keep going against all odds. The reader will not want to put this book down and need to know how the adventure ends as soon as possible. Jost does an amazing job of drawing the reader in with the plot and development of the characters and the story does not disappoint."

—Laura Fowler Paulus, published author and Editor of the Hillsboro Free Press

Asteral's Key was an unexpected delight in every way. With an uncertain outcome, a story that matters, and characters both flawed and courageous, this novel artfully manages to avoid the pitfalls of predictable solutions found all too often in Christian-based fantasy and fiction. The darkness is relentless and will seemingly win the day, yet the small seeds of faith of the characters somehow propel them forward with hope and perseverance in their quest to defeat the enemies that abound and often break their hearts. Packed with action, wisdom, and vivid storytelling, this first novel by Jost pays homage to Tolkien, yet carves out its own niche in the genre.

—Mark Dorn, Professor of Music, Colorado Christian Professor of Music, Colorado Christian University

The Prophecy

Hails starlight

Snows moonlight

Grays twilight

Clears sunlight

Till all rains glass

Within His remnant

Evil shall lament

In the abysmal deep

One's blood will be spilled

Once the Quest is fulfilled

The Star; the divine triad

Will become a New Era; the dyad

So that all evil may pass

When all rains glass

Contents

Prologue

"Dearest Asteral above, we are frightened because the Quest has failed—evil still lurks from the depths." The woman peered out her window at the three-pointed star of their Creator, Asteral. "Every day we wonder why this Key has been entrusted to us, but we know Your plans are good. We have no choice but to entrust the Key to our firstborn. She must succeed where we failed. Please, give my husband the right words to say when the time comes, and surround her with friends who will stand with her along the way. Amen."

"A-amen," mumbled the man, peering into his wife's fading eyes.

She fingered the crystalline Key in her hand. "I hope it's not too late," she whispered, studying the three-pointed star reflected in the transparent Key.

The man clasped his hand in hers. "Are you certain of this? How can you expect our daughter to somehow succeed where we have failed? Do you foresee she will travel all the way to the damned lands of Fhar? The enemy's forces are too strong—even for us."

She withdrew her hand, leaving the Key in his palm. "I want to know why we didn't succeed just as much as you, but we must trust in Him and in the plans He has for us."

The man stared at the Key, glaring at him tauntingly in the starlight. "I—"

"Please, you must give her the Key and instruct her to fulfill the Quest when she's older."

He burst into tears. "'Tis too cruel a burden to inflict on our little girl."

"The Gate must be locked once and for all." Asteral's Remnant reflected in her blue eyes as she murmured:

"The Star; the divine triad
Will become a New Era; the dyad..."

The man finished the statement with glistening eyes:

"...So that all evil may pass
When all rains glass..."

She peered past her husband's gaze, her blue eyes looking beyond the ceiling. "'Tis my dying...wish." Her final breath escaped from her lips. A look of peace washed over her.

"Please—no. You can't..."

The man's tears threatened to strangle him as his thoughts turned to his firstborn and the charge she now must carry. "Oh, daughter, dear, dear daughter, what am I to say to her?" He looked down at the tiny bundle of his stillborn son and considered the burden of grief already heaped upon her.

He peered out the window at the Star of Asteral, shaking with rage. "'Tis too cruel, Asteral. He choked, shouting, "'Tis too cruel!" He had a white-knuckled grip on the Key. He felt the cold crystal pierce his flesh, reminding him of his wife's plea that would haunt him until her final request was fulfilled.

Chapter 1

February 13, 3,285 A.R.

Selest peered through the cottage window at the stars scattered upon a navy canvas. Her hand was pressed against the cool glass.

The sky was bleak, masked in silhouetted pines. Beyond the green-gray needles, she could depict the faintest of stars. Tonight they would shine their brightest upon the plains of Sovoria. Her gaze lowered to the book in her hand. She fingered through the remaining pages, the words on the parchment drawing her into a world where all was once fair and good.

The words danced to an enchanting rhythm in Selest's memory. She closed her eyes and was light as a feather. For a moment, all her burdens were lifted. Her heart warmed as a familiar face crossed her mind.

Mother. Deep longing ached within her, for her mother always read the last paragraph aloud to make sure Selest understood the importance of the passage.

As Selest read, she envisioned the brave Elarael, archangel of Sovoria, facing the witches' wrath. Not heeding her enemy, she peered above at the heavens, seeking Asteral's strength in her darkest hour. When the enemy cut off her wings, Elarael was showered in white light, reborn.

Selest closed the cover. Jealousy tugged at her heart. If only she could write about adventures of her own. Never once had she ventured beyond The Glade. The older she got, the more protective her father had become.

"If only I could be as brave as you, Elarael," she whispered. She leaned back in her chair, staring up thoughtfully.

The etchings on the ceiling turned to constellations of white wings and poisonous daggers in her imagination and made the outside world dull in comparison.

A knock jolted her out of her vision. She quickly opened the door, and her father entered. His blue eyes were twinkling, and his hands were full. "The guests are to arrive shortly, and I need your help carrying the bottles of cider." He chuckled, seeing the familiar book in her hand. "Daydreaming again, I fancy?"

"Yea. 'Tis what I do best," she sighed. "Nothing exciting happens here."

"Well, it is Starry Eve, is it not?" Her father rustled her raven-blue hair. "Ah, come now, Selestial. There'll be a great feast tonight. Songs will be sung. Tales will be told. Fireworks will burst into the starry sky. Tonight will be a night to remember."

She smiled. "I hope you're right, Father."

She followed him down the stairs into the main hall. Grabbing a crate of cider, she stepped out onto the front porch where stars at the peak of dawning made her stop in wonder.

She sighed, wishing she could escape her boring life and fly up to the stars, just like Elarael.

"Selestial, be a dear and set the cider over there," motioned her father.

Sighing, she descended the porch steps and set the crate down. In the distance, the creaking of farm wagons caught her attention. "Father, they're coming."

Savion clasped his hands together. "Ah, perfect timing."

The sound of footsteps and the clomp of hooves rang in her ears as the guests grew closer. Selest found herself surrounded by talk of good tidings and merry jesting. The voices were of many clans: Outdusks, Highdawns, Lownights, Farlights, and above it all, the voice of her father, Savion Inriser. She knew they were all distant relatives, but not one face stood out. Regardless, she forced a smile. After all, she was the daughter of their host.

Wooden benches and chairs dotted the front lawn as people settled for the evening's festivities. A Lownight elder had much difficulty settling into her seat. Selest rushed over to her.

"Here, let me help you." She took the old woman's wrinkly hand.

"Oh thank you, dear. Bless you."

Selest settled into the seat next to her. "Those chairs can be awful tricky if you're not careful."

Elder Lownight snickered. "Your father needs to update these chairs. Tacky furniture indeed. Why, if Arisael were here, she would set him straight."

Selest froze. "With all due respect, ma'am, but my mother's passing was quite recent, and I'd appreciate it if—"

"Oh, cheer up, girl." The lady patted her on the leg. "Asteral never gives us more than we can bear."

The air grew heavy.

"E-excuse me." Selest dashed away to the edge of the crowd, leaving the old woman with her mouth agape. The Elder huffed, and quickly found an Outdusk relative to gossip with.

Selest folded her arms over her chest, rocking back and forth on her heels.

She lifted her gaze to the stars and stretched out her hand, hoping in vain to grasp the warm raiments of her mother.

As if on cue, her father strode before the gathering raising a glass of cider. The conversation gradually faded. Even the wind ceased to blow on such an occasion.

"Hear! Hear!" Savion's voice echoed merrily. "Tonight, we celebrate with a time of song and feasting." Cheers sounded throughout the gathering.

"Here's to good tidings a-many a night!" Everyone raised their glasses in reply and drank until their wits were muddled. Flute and harp led the celebration in the melodious songs of old. Selest smiled when they played a familiar jig from her childhood:

> Lor-Lee-lie-lie-lie
> Lor-Lee-lie-lie-lie
> The same cold breeze
> That rustles the leaves
> Blows forth an icy gale
> Creating spirits soaring free
> Beyond what we could ev'r see
> The same cold breeze
> Amongst the eaves
> Stirs leaf o'er yon' trail
> Telling us who we're meant to be
> Beyond what we could ev'r see
> The same cold breeze
> Of wintry freeze
> Beckons ice and snow to fail
> Bringing forth silver mists o' spring
> Calling ev'ry breath to rise and sing
> The same cold breeze
> Has all the Keys
> So we can unlock the veil
> Revealing who we're meant to be
> Beyond what one did ever see

Wind and dried leaf whirled and twirled with the merry spring reel.

This was Selest's favorite time of year. The clear gray skies looked down on barren tree branches that were just beginning to produce tiny buds. Droplets formed a floral mist around the trees.

She sat on a log on the periphery while everyone danced and sang in merriment beneath the glow of stars and fireworks; they almost seemed a mirage in the cool evening fog.

She sighed. Oh, how the vivid colors shone brightly that magical night. Amidst the splendor, all grew quiet in her mind until a glint of iridescent light caught her eye. "The moon is playing tricks on me," she muttered.

But the closer the light came, the more uncertainty crept into her heart. She gasped as a figure emerged from the eastern pines.

Shadows of needles masked the stranger's face. A faint white light hovered in the air beside him, afloat on a staff of silvery wood—silver oak from the angelic lands of Glascia.

She froze.

He must be one of the angelic folk!

She had never seen an archangel before. In stories, archangels had wings and a haloed crown. This odd being did not bear any of that. The man also seemed too dull to pass as one.

"What are you doing sitting alone in the shadows on this fine holiday?" The stranger's deep voice jolted Selest up from the log. He gave a merry laugh and continued, "Well, 'tis Starry Eve, is it not?"

"W-who and *what* are you, might I ask?"

"Yaelas the Silverin, at your service." He gave a slight bow. "Many paths I have traveled far and wide, but tonight I come to rest my weary feet in The Glade."

"Why here, of all places?" Selest asked, observing him. He wore a robe and a hood; both the same color as his staff.

He paused for a moment, his white beard twitching in the moonlight. "I may have come uninvited, but I am an old friend of your father's. And I bear grave tidings to him and all inhabitants of The Glade."

Her eyes grew wide. "How are you a friend of my father's?" Selest couldn't recall Savion ever mentioning anyone by that name.

Yaelas continued. Either he didn't hear her, or he refused to answer the question—Selest was never sure.

"If you wish to know the news I bring, you can hear along with your kin."

The odd man drew near the gathering. Selest strained to keep up with his long strides. Reluctantly, she joined the crowd. A silent aura weighed heavily upon the merry gathering.

Everyone looked their way, curious about this interruption to the festivities.

"Take heed, villagers of The Glade!" His voice rang as clear as the trumpet of judgment. "I bear dreadful tidings: I have witnessed evil stirring once more. Witches practice evil spells on the borders of the Misty Forest. In the ancient Dwarven Kingdom of Dwindloth, demons lurk. And I say unto you and to your kin, make haste, away! to the Golden Fields of Orai, for the Witches of Shaeel shall return and reclaim their dwelling place of old!"

Murmurs broke the deafening silence. "This is a peaceful gathering, Yaelas. You know you are not welcome here." Her father's voice confronted the man. Selest felt the thick tension in the air between them.

"I came to warn you, Savion, of what is coming, and that I did," replied Yaelas.

"I recognize the likes of him!" shouted one of the Highdawns. "He's a warlock. Nothing but trouble!"

"Indeed," someone else agreed, "we have been at peace for thousands of years. The witches are extinct!"

"Not in this era!" boomed Yaelas. Out of nowhere, thunder shook the earth.

Everyone stumbled to the ground.

"Doom is upon you all!" he declared as he quickly stormed off. What errand urged him speedily onward, none could tell. He was but a phantom in the shadows along the Lone Road.

Selest didn't receive any answers that night or the day after. Her father and the rest of the family refused to talk about the stranger or the strange events of that Starry Eve.

It was a night to remember indeed.

Chapter 2

Three years later

The crescent moon gleamed down upon Selest as she walked along the line of dimly lit trees. Their branches strained to grasp the radiance of the moon's rays. But instead of yearning to reach the orb's timeless face, Selest peered at the cold engravings etched in the cool granite. The family burial site greeted her with a sorrowful welcome.

Arisael Inriser, Beloved Mother
& Savion II, Beloved Son and
Brother, Stillborn.
Died September 15, 3,284 A.R.

Her lungs tightened as she tried to release a sigh.

Four years had passed: four long, never-ending years.

A lump formed in her throat.

Beyond the headstone, the gloomy night would soon shut the eyes of the day.

Selest got to her feet as the world spun before her. She steadied herself against the stone.

Through her tears, she deciphered the outline of her home a hundred yards away.

The sound of hooves was distant in her ears but she paid little heed. Traders always came down from the Misty Forest to barter goods in Snowtown.

The sound grew louder. Curiosity got the best of her.

As she stole a glance, she gasped in terror. A muscular steed towered menacingly above her. Its coat was blacker than night itself, mane and tail whipping like phantoms in the wind.

Red eyes glared into her soul. Her heart nearly leaped from her throat.

A kelpie!

She dared a peek at its master. The figure was clad with a cape and hood. No face was visible.

Her heart caught in her throat. *It must be a Shadower!*

Only in stories did she hear of their menacing presence.

She shrank away, knees buckling.

The wind whipped the figure's cape as she discerned the shape of a sword. She trembled. The ghastly figure withdrew its hood.

Selest beheld the face of a young man, weather-beaten from travel. His gray eyes were full of concern. His beard twitched in the biting cold, and his kelpie snorted in irritation. He dismounted, hands raised. "Don't be frightened, lass. I don't mean to do you any harm."

"W-who are you?" she asked, slowly regaining her composure.

"I am Thrion, son of Yaelas the Silveran, at your service." He bowed. "I am but a messenger from the Misty Forest. I come as a bearer of news, as well as a weary traveler seeking shelter and good food for the evening."

"Yaelas," she whispered. "The one who came to warn us all those years ago?"

He nodded. "What is your name?"

"Before I answer, tell me this—where does your allegiance lie?"

"My allegiance lies in no earthly figure, but in Asteral alone."

She relaxed. If his faith was intact, surely he was trustworthy.

"My name you have won. I am Selestial Inriser, daughter to Savion."

"A pleasure, Selestial." He bowed once more, gesturing at his steed. "And this is my companion, Wraith."

The morbid creature glared as if trying to intimidate her.

She shivered. "Forgive me, but why do you keep a kelpie as your steed?"

Thrion scratched the stallion behind the ears. "I tamed him as a foal from the Emen Marshes near the Misty Forest. He bears no affiliation with agents of evil."

She shivered. Her fancies must've gotten the better of her.

"Y-you said you had news to share with my family?"

"I do."

She shivered. It was likely the same news Yaelas bore all those years ago.

He pulled his hood over his head. "You best tell your father of my coming, lass."

Selest started toward her home.

"May I ask who is buried there?" Thrion said.

Selest came to an abrupt halt. Turning, she simply replied. "My mother and brother."

Thrion's gaze softened. "I can only imagine what it felt like losing two whom you loved so dearly." He softly added, "My mother died when I was a lad."

She winced. How terrible that must have felt.

Selest bowed her head. "Forgive me, but you were not what I expected."

Bewilderment etched his features. "Oh?"

She felt her face turning red. "I—I mistook you for a Shadower at first glance."

The man's gaze softened. "Again, I'm sorry for frightening you, but please rest assured I will not harm you."

She sighed. "Follow me."

Selest led him to the front porch of the cottage.

She wrung her apron. "My father is inside. He's not expecting company." Quickly, she added, "I am not sure how he will react to your presence. He did not take too kindly to your father all those years ago."

Thrion paused. "Relay what I've told you. Tell him I come in the name of our Creator." He turned, "Where can I keep my steed?"

Selest pointed at the barn.

Thrion turned, leading Wraith. "I shan't be too long then."

Selest went up the porch steps and turned the iron knob. The oaken door creaked open. "Father? Are you here?"

Her father approached, cleaning his butchering knife with a rag. "Ah, Selest. Were the graves as well-kept as last time?"

"Yes, sir. While I paid a visit, I ran into a passerby. He bears news, and he wishes to seek shelter for the night."

Savion went to the window. "He is tending to his steed," she continued. "He should come shortly. His name is Thrion, son of Yaelas—"

"Yaelas?" Savion's expression grew dark.

"F-father, listen…" she stammered as he stormed outside.

She rushed after him. "He brings no harm. He comes in the name of Asteral."

Before she could say more, Thrion approached from the barn.

Savion stood protectively before his daughter, knife in hand. "You're Yaelas' son?"

"Yes, sir. I presume your daughter told you my reason for coming?"

"My daughter told me enough of you," he said in a bitter tone. He pointed his knife threateningly. "I want you to fetch your steed and leave this peaceful village."

"Stay your weapon, sir. I haven't come to disrupt peace, but to relay vital news. Would you not take kindly to a stranger and welcome him into your home?"

Selest grasped her father's hand. "It would be of ill conduct not to welcome a godly stranger."

Savion paused. "Alas, fear has gotten the better of me."

Thrion approached. "One can't be too careful in these trying times."

Savion pointed to the house, "Come, let us start anew."

As they went inside, Savion led the way to the dining room. A long table stood in the middle to their right; the chairs on either side were perfectly aligned.

"Would you like something to eat?" Selest pulled out a chair for him.

Thrion accepted the seat. "I would be obliged, thank you."

Selest sliced a block of nutty-flavored cheese and stuffed it in a loaf of oat bread topped with a slab of butter and a dab of apple cider jam.

She brought the food and set it before him.

"Would you care for some mulled wine? I still think we have a crate or two from Yule."

"Why yes, thank you."

Selest looked in the cupboard. Empty.

She turned to her father. "Let me fetch some from the cellar. I shan't be too long." With that, she left the two men talking about strange doings throughout the Inner Realm.

Fetching a lantern she walked through the kitchen exiting into the night.

She strolled over a dimly lit stone trail with the waxing crescent as her guide.

The wooden door of the cellar finally came into view. All was deathly quiet and she grew increasingly uneasy.

With a trembling hand, she swung open the door. Before her, the cavernous maw gaped—a kind of dark without a speck of light. Just emptiness.

Tonight she had to face her fears. Taking a deep breath, she crept down the wooden ladder. The planks creaked in protest bearing her slight weight. When her feet hit the ground, a putrid odor assaulted her.

She held her breath and held up the lantern. The darkness reluctantly gave way to the faint orange glow.

Selest determined the outline of crates and barrels in disarray.

She scouted the crates with wine. A glint of glass caught her eye.

As quietly as deep waters flow she approached, carefully trying to withdraw a bottle. If one crate or barrel was misplaced, the gigantic heap would consume her.

Sweat erupted from her brow as the bottle refused to budge.

One yank was all it would take—just one. Eerily, the wind picked up. The cellar door slammed. Selest leaped from her skin, taking the bottle with her.

The mighty heap came tumbling down. Fearing for her life, she sprang upright and dashed for the ladder. She leaped upon the rungs. A crate's sharp end grazed her shoulder. She scrambled upward, yearning for moonlight, when a hiss of death sounded from behind her.

Fear crept up her spine. She dared a glance back. Behind the chaotic pile, a shadow lay outstretched. Her eyes widened. The odor was stronger than ever, sending tears down her face. She beheld the visage of a cow skull hanging upon a specter draped in black cloth. Its gaping eyes bore into her soul. Its cartilage was stained in blood. Black tears streamed down its face.

AH!

A scream escaped from her lips. A bloodcurdling cackle matched her volume of terror. Selest turned away and scrambled up the ladder. She threw herself at the door and fell face-first. She scrambled to her feet as the sound grew closer.

She dashed madly for the house. She tripped up the steps and slammed the door behind her.

Her life flashed before her eyes at that moment as a daze turned to reality. She feared the worst was yet to come.

Father. She needed Father.

She crashed into someone. The bottle of wine still glued to her hand dropped to the floor and shattered.

She let out a sob, trembling uncontrollably.

"Selestial, what happened?" Savion embraced his daughter. She buried her head in his tunic, trying to unsee the horror.

"Witch!" she rasped. "Witch!"

Thrion approached and placed a hand on each of their shoulders. "Listen, both of you. My father is evacuating other Western refugees as we speak. I was sent to warn The Glade. Yaelas shall meet us at the House of Orai. I advise you to journey there as well. The yearly Council is being held in a few months. If we go now, we can reach them, and tell them of the stirring of evil in the West. Let us make haste, for this place is no longer safe. The witches are gathering. I fear we're outnumbered."

Savion shook his fist at Thrion.

"You expect us to travel all the way to Orai, through the Fields of Shile, and across the frozen pass of Glasefell? It's too dangerous."

"So is remaining here. Think of your daughter's safety."

Savion stroked Selest's hair.

After a moment of silence, Savion asked, "Have you warned the other residents?"

Thrion lowered his gaze. "Yes. I fear it's too late for them."

Savion trembled. "For too long we've let the comforts of home disillusion us with the thought of peace."

Screaming came from outside. Thrion turned to them. "We must evacuate *now*."

Chapter 3

Thrion unsheathed his sword and looked both in the eye, his expression firm.

Silence hung as a veil, draping them all with gloom.

Selest's breath caught in her throat as she feared the worst.

Her eyes were fixed on her father in horror.

Urgency flashed through his eyes. "This way." He led them past the dining room and into the hallway.

Savion was silent. He peered at a painting of Arisael. Her wavy hair was as black as the silken feathers of a crow shimmering in the starlight; her sapphire eyes were caring and wise.

"Father?" Selest crept to the edge of the hall. Grief besieged her heart, as she too peered at the portrait of her mother. Her father had never gotten over the death of his wife and son.

Slowly, he turned to her. "Selestial, when your mother and brother died—" His voice broke. "There is something I want you to have."

He reached into his pocket and retrieved a Key forged of the purest crystal. The colors reflected upon it as if from an unearthly source; even in that grave moment, Selest was captured in its unnatural beauty.

She felt time stop. How could something so unearthly be his to bear?

Savion took Selest's hand and placed the Key firmly in her palm. He traced the outline of the Key thoughtfully with a finger.

"In ancient days the Key of Ezelex was forged to keep the door to the Devil's lair sealed. But the door was opened by those who swore to keep the Key safe from selfish desires. Now the door must be sealed once more. 'Tis said one of good faith would bear it to the land of Fhar and lock the door once more so that evil would be vanquished from the Inner Realm."

Selest couldn't believe what she was hearing. Of all people, how had her father come by this?

Savion squeezed her hand. "'Twas your mother's. She gave it to me before she passed. 'Twas her dying wish to see this Quest fulfilled."

"If that is what I think it is, then if the witches find it they will kill us all," Thrion hissed.

"Why did you keep this from me if it was her dying wish?" cried Selest. "Now the whole world is in grave danger!"

"We must bring it forth to Yaelas in Orai," Thrion declared. "This Key could be the answer to ending this siege. You have all the more reason to journey there."

"The witches will hunt us down on the road," Selest countered.

After much consideration, Savion peered at his daughter with a sad expression. "Then I shall remain here."

"Father—no." The thought of it engulfed her. She felt the weight of bereavement she had only experienced when she lost her mother. Savion wrapped his arms lovingly around his daughter. "I am old, Selestial. I will not make the journey."

She peered into his eyes, searching for an answer in their brown depths. "Father, why—?"

"The witches are rallying. If I can stall them—"

"No, Father, no." She shook her head violently.

"If the Key is what they seek, then they will presume I have it. My remaining here gives you and Thrion time to escape."

"No!" she screamed.

Suddenly, they heard the shattering of glass. A hiss echoed throughout the house.

Hhhggggg...

Savion turned to Thrion. "Protect her."

The man gave a firm nod. "I will."

Savion's gaze pierced through his daughter's heart. With trembling hands, he grabbed hers, both hands entwining the Key. "Fulfill the good of this earth," he looked into her dark eyes for the last time, "for in Asteral we shall be reborn."

He let go of her hands.

Thrion seized Selest by the shoulders, "Come, Selest." He urged her up the staircase that lay before them.

"Father—" She tried to escape the stranger's grasp with every ounce of strength she could muster. But Thrion held firm.

"Father!" she yelled.

With one final sorrowful look at her, Savion turned and faced the oncoming foe. He unsheathed his dagger, bracing for whatever was to come. His expression remained peaceful, knowing he did what he could for his family and knowing that was enough. When the first witch approached, Thrion pushed Selest up the steps, unsheathing his sword and following after her.

Savion sounded a battle cry, dagger raised high. With all the strength he possessed, he charged the first witch, beheading the foul creature. More came; he held his ground.

As if in a dream, her reality shattered, Selest found herself crossing the small hallway to her room.

With much haste, Thrion went to the window where her desk stood. He leaped atop it and threw open the window.

As quiet as a windless night, he climbed onto the shingled roof. Selest remained where she was, unmoving. Thrion reached through the window, seizing her by the shoulders and drawing her onto the slanting roof. They were engulfed within the black sky dotted by the tiny cold lights of stars.

Slowly their eyes adjusted to the blackness as they heard piercing cries from below carried on the howling wind.

Thrion slid to the ledge of the rooftop. The drop was only a few feet downward. He pulled Selest with him. She slipped on the tiles damp from the cool air. She saw her life flash before her eyes as she doubled over in fear, afraid she would be eaten alive by many unseen ghouls.

Thrion's grip remained firm. She reeled back, gulping for air. When he was certain not a soul was nearby, he seized his chance.

He inched another couple of feet to the left and jumped to the ground. He gestured for Selest to do the same.

She froze. If she jumped off this roof now, there was no return. But if she remained, she could help her father. Her decision was made. She climbed back up the roof as Thrion called after her. Her fingers grabbed the window ledge when a voice echoed within her mind.

Fulfill the good of this earth…

Fresh tears streamed down her face.

Would she be doing that by returning to her father, who meant to sacrifice his life for her? By leaving her mother's dying wish unfulfilled?

Taking a deep breath, she slid down the roof once more, and with one look at Thrion, she hesitated. Finally, she leaped into his arms.

"I am glad you chose wisely," Thrion said. He seized her hand, and they both sprinted across the clearing away from her house and into the barn.

An ear-splitting shriek sounded from the house. It wasn't the morbid hiss of a witch, but a cry of pure fear. Thrion and Selest looked at the house.

Realization struck Selest like a cold front slamming down upon the warmth of the earth.

"No!" she sank to the ground in tears, joining her father's grievous cries.

Quickly, Thrion saddled Wraith and swung astride.

He leaned down and called, "Selest, get on!"

She tried, but grief crippled her. She found herself yanked off her feet. Astride Wraith, she peered beyond the horse's shadowed head at what lay before them.

Dim figures raced in their direction sounding a bloody cry. She lost herself in the bottomless pit of their gaping eyes.

Thrion placed a protective arm around her. "Yah!" He pulled hard on the reins.

The kelpie reared, hooves clawing the air. Wraith then kicked off at full speed. Their surroundings blurred. The horror pressed against their backs. Soon the deafening cries and the shadow of Selest's home were lost.

Chapter 4

Selest huddled against the warmth of Thrion's cloak, sobbing. "Why didn't we listen?" she kept repeating. "Why?" She was lost in a pool of grief.

Through scratchy eyes, Selest peered at the purple dawn lighting the endless path that lay ahead. She ached as sobs wracked her body.

It didn't feel real—it couldn't be. The wind sliced through her thick dress like a knife, sending shivers throughout her body. She felt the Key embedded in the frozen skin of her hand. In spite of everything that had transpired the night before, she had held onto it.

She felt the ghastly beast panting heavily, bearing the burden of many miles.

"Whoa." Thrion quietly coaxed him to a halt near a single oak apart from the ancient hedge. Its branches extended with welcoming arms, sheltering them against the biting arctic wind.

Thrion dismounted and scouted the area while Selest remained in the saddle.

Her body was stiff. So stiff that she felt herself falling from the mount. Thrion caught her just before she hit the ground. "Are you all right?" He eyed her with concern.

She didn't answer. Thrion settled her to rest against the tree. He unclasped his cape and wrapped it tightly around her. He then led Wraith further behind the boughs of another gnarled tree hidden from the road.

He tied the reins to a sturdy branch and sat down on the floor of fallen leaves that rustled in the howling wind.

Thrion retrieved a map from his saddlebag. "We're well over fifty miles from The Glade, considering how we've ridden all night. With the pace we're going we should reach the borders of Snowtown within the next week or two, maybe more. But we have outrun the witches; I dare hope for good for the time being. We can stop here for a quick breakfast."

She shivered.

Between the Gladen Lands and Snowtown, the Lone Road cut across the forsaken Fields of Shile.

Those lands were forbidden to pass through.

Selest isolated herself from the gray world, staring at the fallen leaves not yet restored by the coming of spring.

Wraith nosed through patches of snow nearby, munching on the shriveled grass.

Thrion leaned over and fetched something from the saddlebag.

A glint of red caught the corner of Selest's eye. "Hungry?"

Selest felt her stomach growl as she took the apple absentmindedly.

Thrion rose, scouting the area. "We should be safe for the time being. I shall have to resupply our food and water before we depart."

Selest said nothing, staring at the apple.

Satisfied that their camp was hidden from strangers or foes approaching on the road, Thrion went hunting for game, leaving Selest alone.

The icy wind sliced through her dress. She wrapped the hunter's cloak tightly around her as she nibbled on the apple.

She leaned back harder and harder against the tree hoping to escape the wind's wrath. Suddenly, she felt the tree cave in. She found her upper half lying in the hollow interior of the tree.

She scrambled out of the hollow and turned to inspect it. As she got a closer look, it appeared larger than she thought.

The floor was matted with dry animal droppings and fresh dirt. Nothing stirred therein. Selest crawled into the cavity and rested against the bark. As she stared into the window of blinding gray sky, she pressed her hands against her dress pocket where her Key was, as though the trinket would warm her hands.

She sat there, numbed by cold and grief until the howling wind lulled her into a dreamless sleep.

When she awoke, the blinding gray had turned to a dreary blue. All was deathly still.

She noticed her eyes had adjusted to the dark burrow. As she peered at the oaken walls, she noticed symbols carved into the bark.

She squinted. It was a type of writing she couldn't decipher. She shifted uneasily.

Who could've lived here? Certainly not animals. They couldn't write such intricate signs.

Her heart quickened. "Thrion?" her voice cracked. "Thrion?" she repeated, louder.

She felt her hand brush against something hairy. She recoiled as if she'd been stung.

Her eyes widened. To her horror she saw a head with gaping eyes staring at her. If it was a witch or a man she couldn't tell. Immediately that place of comfort turned into a place of horror. It was like being in the cellar all over again.

Gasping, she scrambled from the comfort of the hollow and out into the biting cold.

"Selest!"

She froze. Did her ears deceive her? Was the ghastly creature calling her name?

Turning, she saw Thrion with a deer slung over his shoulder. He dropped his prize and rushed to her, brow furrowed.

He examined her. "Are you all right? What happened?"

She pointed a shaking hand at the hollow. "There's someone in there."

Selest explained how she discovered the hollow and the odd symbols.

Thrion drew his sword, advancing toward the oak. As he peered inside, Selest clung to the folds of her apron.

Thrion later retreated. "Whoever it was, they've been dead for a while. No doubt a victim of the Wiccan spell."

Selest held her hand to her mouth. "I took shelter in a witch's lair?"

Thrion led Selest to Wraith. "Hidden Hollows were commonplace amongst witches for a time. You were just unfortunate enough to stumble upon one, lass."

Fear rattled her bones. "Let's leave this place," she whispered.

"Agreed." With that, Thrion packed up the game and they mounted Wraith, continuing on their journey.

Neither spoke a word. All that could be heard was the desolate wind.

As the evening got darker, it grew colder. This made Selest all the more grateful for Thrion's cloak.

"How are you faring?" he asked.

"I'm managing," she said quietly, snuggling in the cloak tightly. "I thank you for your kindness, Thrion."

He wrapped his arm around her as they settled into a trot.

The watchful night closed in. She peered at the crescent moon cast in the deep pools of night. They stopped to rest once more.

Sighing, she lay down on the freezing ground, and though part of the moon hid its face in the night's veil, she saw the same mystical and timeless moon that ever shone during those Starry Eves. The same cold breeze rustling the leaves swirled about her.

She found herself singing a song from a long time ago.

The same cold breeze
That rustles the leaves
Blows forth an icy gale
Creating spirits soaring free
Beyond what we could ev'r see

She was finally carried off into a dream-filled sleep of twirling leaves and a cold familiar breeze.

Thrion remained awake and alert, his hand tracing the carven hilt of his sword.

But nothing unexpected happened that night.

Selest awoke to the smell of roasted deer. Her mouth watered. For the first time in a while, she had an appetite. After a quiet breakfast, they continued once more along the Lone Road.

Along the way, the gray plains about them remained true in the light of a pale sun over a new, misty morn.

Selest sat astride Wraith, peering straight ahead, wondering what adventures lay beyond.

"H-how are you, Selest?" Thrion asked, startling her from her thoughts.

"Hm?" She glanced down from her mount. Thrion walked alongside Wraith.

Thrion gave a light laugh. "Not much of a conversationalist, eh?"

"O-oh. N-no, not really. I'm thinking about what lies ahead. I–I've never ventured outside of The Glade before."

Thrion furrowed his brow. "Really?"

"Yes." Selest placed a hand over her pocket. "That's why I've always read books, yearning for adventures of my own. At the same time, I feel betrayed—"

Inhaling a shaky breath she choked on the words she'd been meaning to say, "Have we really been so disillusioned with peace that we failed to acknowledge the witches coming? Why did my father keep the knowledge of the Key from me? Did he think I couldn't bear it?"

Unexpectedly, she heard Thrion say, "I do not know why. But this I do know: Cry as long as the sun sets and the moon rises, for you are weak."

Then he turned and met her dark eyes.

"But weakness shall make you stronger."

She felt a calming presence wash over her.

"Have faith, dear heart," Thrion said, his gray eyes twinkling in the morning light.

Sighing, Selest thought back on all that had happened. She knew deep down she still grieved for the death of her family and for The Glade. But she also knew they would want her to be happy. And knowing that was enough.

"Let us fulfill this Quest. Succeed or not, we shall endure. We've made it this far," Selest proclaimed.

"That we shall," replied Thrion.

Days passed slowly as the cold air of winter overtook them. The Lone Road seemed all the more endless ahead.

One day, snow clouds masked the noon sun as white flakes fell down on the weary travelers freezing them to the bone. It sent forth a penetrating numbness that seeped into their skin. Plodding along in the snow, an outline of trees appeared to their right. At first, it seemed a silvery mirage shimmering in the fog. But as they drew nearer the mirage solidified and the gray curtain gave way.

A feeling of dread overwhelmed Selest as she peered into the hypnotic depths of the grove.

"Thrion, why is that forest so enchanting?" Her eyes remained glued to the orchard.

Astride the kelpie, Thrion urged the steed forward, wanting to go at a quicker pace before the reign of night. Instead, Wraith came to an abrupt halt. A distinguishing scent was in the air. He grew restless, prancing in place.

"Whoa, easy now," Thrion said.

But the kelpie's eyes glowed as red as a blood moon.

"Does Wraith sense danger?" asked Selest.

"Yes, I imagine, but I cannot be sure what it is with the density of the fog."

The snow began to pile up at an alarming rate. The fog enshrouded them like a thick blanket, obscuring their surroundings. They could only trust the keen senses of the kelpie now.

Thrion and Selest squinted in the direction of the kelpie's gaze.

They heard the sound of footsteps crunching on the ice. Someone or something drew near.

Whatever it was, it upset the kelpie a good deal, and they knew that could be a nasty business to get caught up in. Thrion came to an abrupt halt and swung off his steed. He unsheathed his sword and took a fighting stance. "Selest, remain where you are," he said over his shoulder. Astride Wraith, Selest felt the kelpie prance in agitation.

"Thrion, be care—"

A sudden force knocked Thrion off his feet.

The misty curtain rolled back, revealing a golden blur.

The kelpie reared, his hooves clawing viciously at the air. He whistled his challenge to his foe.

Selest had a white-knuckled grip on Wraith's mane as he struck the snow-packed earth and began to charge.

All she could do was remain astride, holding on for dear life.

The attacker seized its chance. It twisted around, lashing out its hind legs with unearthly strength and kicking the kelpie off its hooves. Simultaneously, the great beast swung its lance low beneath Thrion's strike, disarming him instantly.

As the kelpie fell, Selest leaped from the saddle to avoid being crushed on impact. She landed sprawled on hands and knees on the frozen ground.

Thrion lay there stunned. What could take out a kelpie and a hunter in a single strike?

The powerful warrior landed with stealth. In the parted fog they beheld a mighty centaur. His hide glistened gold as droplets crystallized on his coat, making him shine like the sun in the colorless landscape. He towered over them menacingly. Slowly, Selest peered up into his maple-brown eyes.

In awe, Thrion forgot he still had his sword drawn. "Lay down your weapon," hissed the centaur as cold as the blade he wielded, "or you shall die."

"Stop!" Selest, sore and freezing, stumbled between Thrion and the centaur. "Please. Don't hurt us." She trembled.

The centaur withdrew. His expression changed from battle-hardened to tender.

He trotted to her side and knelt. "Where do you dwell, child?"

"Th-The Glade."

"That place is crawling with witches." He bowed his head. "Alas, not many survived. Are you injured?"

"No." She tried to stand but stumbled. "Grief has taken a toll on me."

"I can see that." The centaur helped her to her feet.

"What you need is a roaring fire, warm food, and drink in your belly," he said. "I am sorry I startled you."

Thrion rose. "I pray you mistook us for a witch or a Wanderer then, and do not deem us as foe?"

He pointed his sword at Thrion.

"Wait!" she said in a panic. "He's with me."

He glared at Thrion. "If I deemed you as a foe, you would be dead."

The icy wind whipped across the path, slicing through their skin with ferocity.

"Friend or not, we seek shelter for the night. Could you provide that?" Thrion asked.

The centaur eyed the travel-stained man. "Come then, if that's what you seek."

He neared the fallen stallion, standing before it. "As much as I despise these foul creatures, I will be sure to treat his wound."

A nasty cut ran down Wraith's chest.

The fog swirled about them blown by a slight breeze. Selest wrapped herself tighter in the cloak.

Thrion urged the kelpie upward and followed the centaur.

The gray blanket parted, revealing an ancient hedge. Cold needles of fear pricked down her spine. "You live near the borders of Shile?"

"Indeed," the centaur replied. "The lands east of the Emerald Dells are not habitable, even for me."

Wanderers dwelt in the Fields of Shile. A path unfolded before them, and they knew that any who strayed from the path would become a Wanderer themselves. If one ever bore this fate, they would roam the fields, forever lost in another world, never finding what they seek.

The centaur led them off the road, onto a carpet of damp pine needles, and into a grove. After a short while, the trees gave way to a clearing in a sudden rise in the flat earth. From the hill shone an orange hole.

Before them lay a cave. The orange glow of torchlight etched the opening.

Inside, the cave was spacious; the walls gleamed in the torchlight. Selest felt like she was being given a friendly welcome, especially compared to the gloomy land outside.

Selest settled on a nearby cot close to the fire and warmed herself from head to toe.

"Welcome to my home. 'Tis not much, but it shall do."

"Thank you," Thrion said.

"Yes, thank you," said Selest.

"What is your name, if you would be kind enough to give it to us?" Thrion asked.

"Faern Dawnback, son of Faeodin, at your service." He bowed by kneeling on his front hooves with a sweep of his hand. Thrion bowed in reply.

"Thrion the Silveran, at yours."

"Silveran?" Faern asked, a hint of suspicion in his voice.

"I am just a mere hunter. My surname belongs to Yaelas, my father."

The centaur peered at the man. "Now that you mention it, your eyes hold a resemblance."

"You know him?" Thrion asked.

"Indeed," Faern replied. "He fought with my grandfather, Dajen, in the Shadow War years ago. An alliance between my kin and the angels was made. They were marching to the realm of the Fallen. There, they were ambushed by demons. All would have been slaughtered if it weren't for Yaelas coming to their aid. He led the charge and drove those foul creatures to their deaths."

"Yes, he is an extraordinary man," Thrion mumbled mostly to himself.

"And who are you, dear one?" asked Faern.

"I am Selestial Inriser, d-daughter of—" her voice quivered and she whispered, "Savion."

Silence hung like a shroud.

"Her father was slain by the Witches of Shaeel," Thrion explained.

The centaur raised an eyebrow, a look of empathy in his eyes. "I am sorry, I didn't mean to make you upset," he said. "I will get you both something to eat."

The centaur retreated into a nearby room, returned with soup, and gave it to them. He gestured to the right, "Clothes, blankets, and bandages are there. You may help yourselves while I tend to the beast's wound."

He trotted off, leaving the two companions in silence while they ate.

In the midst of the silence, the weight deep within her pocket grew until it became unbearable. She withdrew the Key, examining it, transfixed at the color of torchlight that was mirrored in the crystal depths.

She traced the Key's shape, outlining the ancient engravings of the meticulous portraits that were displayed in the crystal.

"Selest—?"

An echo sounded in the depths of her mind. It grew nearer.

"Selest!" She felt a tap on her shoulder.

Her enthrallment broken, she jerked her head and found herself facing Thrion.

His expression was full of questions.

She had been completely unaware of anyone else's presence.

"You've been staring at that for a while now."

"O-oh." She started, glancing from the Key to Thrion's concerned expression. "I just was taken by the sight of it, that's all."

"Selest," Thrion placed a concerned hand on her shoulder, "you must be careful."

Faern drew near. He stood there awkwardly, not knowing what to make of this situation. Seeing the girl's head bowed, and Thrion comforting her, he walked cautiously to them. "Are you all right?"

Thrion and Selest were startled at the sound of his voice.

Faern halted as the expression on his face became like a stormcloud at the sight of the Key.

Selest froze. Why had she felt the need to fetch the Key now of all times?

Her chest heaved uneasily. The enemy was upon them, and if this centaur was in the same boat as they, didn't he have a right to know?

She turned to face the centaur's shocked gaze. Taking a deep breath, she stared past the large figure to a nearby torch with sparks popping and sizzling. Finally, she said, "I bear the Key of Ezelex."

A heavy silence filled the room.

After a moment or two Faern found the words and asked, "H-how is this yours to bear, child?"

"'Twas my father's." She paused. "This was given to me ere he passed." Silent tears streamed down her face.

"I am deeply sorry," Faern said with empathy. "But how did he come upon it?"

"I—I do not know." She peered up at the rocky ceiling, praying Asteral would give her strength to face whatever lay ahead. "This is why I hope for answers at the House of Orai."

"So that is where you are heading," he mused. "Whom do you seek?"

"My father awaits us there," Thrion said.

Faern furrowed his brow. "For too long these damned fiends have been hiding, and now I see they are more determined than ever to reclaim the Forests of Old," he said.

"Indeed," replied Thrion, "'twas why he told me to make haste west-bound, to warn those who reside there of the witches' return to haunt the forest and The Glade beyond. And for me and those willing to follow to journey to the Golden Sea in the presence of the Grand Council."

All was quiet once more except for the howling wind.

Finally, Selest spoke. "I was the only one willing to follow him."

"So that is how you came to journey together?" asked Faern.

Selest explained the events of that horrific night. How it haunted her, even just speaking of it.

"We rode off in the dead of night onto the Lone Road, all those weeks ago," she finally concluded.

Faern peered at each of them in turn, his eyes full of sadness. "I am deeply sorry for the harrowing losses you have endured."

Selest warmed at his empathy.

Selest and Thrion retrieved clothes, blankets, and bandages and changed in nearby rooms. When they returned, Faern spoke. "I am curious—so you have yet to trek across the Fields of Shile to Snowtown, across the White Mountains, and pass through the Enchanted Forest to reach your destination?"

"That is correct," Thrion said. "My father said in Snowtown there is a church where we could be safe for the time being. A friend of his will aid us. Father Zyon I believe is his name."

"I see." He paused, staring at the floor with his hand pressed to his chin. Finally, he turned and faced Thrion. "Do you know the way?"

"By the path and the guidance of the stars I do. But beyond the White Mountains, I am unsure of the route," Thrion replied.

Faern took this into deep consideration. "I have dwelled in these parts all my life. And now upon hearing the witches have returned beyond, I must seek wisdom from the Great Council regarding this spreading evil. I fear it will not be safe to remain here any longer."

"What are you saying?" Selest asked.

"I will accompany you on your journey."

Chapter 5

At daybreak they arose and began their flight down the path that stretched out before them, etched in the mist cast by the silvering light of dawn.

Refreshed and renewed in their new attire, and after a good breakfast, they continued along the thinning hedge.

Along the way, Thrion and Selest gazed in wonder at the sight before them. In spite of winter's harshness, the hills were a brilliant green—as green as an emerald that was cast with a tinge of silver. It was no wonder that place was known as the Emerald Dells.

Soft rolling hills stretched out before them as far as the eye could see. As they came to an end, the path led to the Fields that lay ahead.

The thought of passing through the fields of Shile sent shivers down their spines. Faern came to a sudden halt. Thrion and Selest halted next to him astride Wraith.

The landscape abruptly changed from a brilliant emerald to a sickly gray. Their eyes were fixed upon the gray earth that seemed to run into the sky. An old ailing hedge was near the road to their right. "Whatever happens, do not stray from the path," Faern warned. "They will try to draw you in amidst the silence. Do not heed them or else you will be in grave danger."

"We already are in grave danger," Selest whispered. Fear grew within her—the same fear that besieged each of them.

"There is no turning back," Thrion whispered in reply.

"Stay close," Faern said.

And with that, they crept closer to the border of the field feeling as if they were meeting certain doom.

An eerie wind blew through the dead leaves creating a ghostly howl that enveloped the land.

Then all sound stopped; the silence was deafening. They could barely make out ghostly figures gliding in the mist as if floating in a dream. The Wanderers were surreal to their eyes.

The fields were dotted with them wandering aimlessly about. The very loneliness sunk deeper through the weary travelers' skin sending shivers down their spines. The Wanderer closest to the road wore a tattered gray hood like a visor; no face was discernible.

A sudden trance overcame Thrion. He dismounted, stepping closer to the fields until he was on the edge of the road.

"*THRION!*" Selest shouted.

Faern heard the girl's plea and spotted the hunter taking another step off the path.

"Thrion, no!" Selest shouted, as frantic as ever.

Faern leaped behind him, yanking him by the arm. Thrion landed sprawled upon his back. "Control yourself, man!" Faern demanded. "They are trying to draw you in." He looked at each intensely in turn. "Resist, lest you desire to become one of *them*."

Selest felt a chill down her spine as her eyes trailed to the nearby Wanderer who was as close as ever to the road. "Do not stare!" Faern hissed. "Do not let them get to you."

Thrion looked down at the ground, panting. The same haunted expression Selest had was reflected in his eyes.

"Come, let us move ahead," the centaur said as he gestured onward.

They journeyed on in the eerie silence. Thousands upon thousands of lost souls swirled around them.

"We are almost to the end," Faern declared, his voice like a crack of thunder before the breaking of a storm.

At that moment, a hiss colder than a winter's night pierced the screaming silence.

Hhhhhhhhh...

A witch cry it was not, for it was heavier; more akin to the whistling wind.

Thrion froze. "'Tis no Wanderer." A bolt of realization struck. "Shadowers are amongst them."

The small party stopped in their tracks. "Impossible," whispered Faern.

Everyone knew the tale. It was said that Shadowers were Nephilims who were once guards of the Key that Selest possessed. These angelic guards were overcome with temptation and thus cursed to roam the Inner Realm. Known as the Eleven, the Shadowers were the only ones who could step upon the path to trap their victims.

Selest turned this way and that, trying to see any sign of them. Then to her horror she saw footsteps embedded in the gray soil along the side of the trail.

Eyes wide, she stuttered, "Th-there are footprints."

Thrion and Faern turned to where she gazed.

"They are near." Faern drew his lance, peering beyond the prints.

Thrion drew his broadsword. He strained to hear their cold hiss, but only the kelpie's sensitive ears were keen enough to detect it.

These fields were where Wraith's ancestors dwelled; they were calling the great beast to come forth into the blackened wastelands from whence his ancestors came.

Hhhhhhhhhhss—

The wretched cry sounded nearby, but the Eleven were invisible to all. The kelpie grew restless, stomping in place; the call to him was strong.

Selest froze, afraid of what the beast might do. Wraith reared, whistling his challenge in reply to the Fields, trying to resist the burning temptation. The kelpie's shrill whistle pierced Selest's very essence as she held onto its mane for dear life. But the motion threw her onto the ground with a *thud!*

She lay there, her body screaming with pain. Her world slowly blurred when an echo sounded in the void of her mind.

"Selest!" Footsteps pounded her way. Even that sound hurt.

She groaned in protest trying to rise, but pain seized her like invisible hands holding her to the ground.

She felt a strange weight within her. She grasped at her pocket and traced the shape of the Key with a cold finger as it seemed to pulse to the beat of her pounding heart.

Wraith galloped madly across the road and into the fields, the calling too much for him to resist. He was forever lost.

The Shadowers followed Wraith's cries and charged the group astride kelpies of their own with daggers raised.

Time seemed to stop at that moment. The Shadowers charged them— but why? Were they after the Key? Could they somehow sense it?

Her father had possessed it, and that was all she knew. All else died away with him, his blood on the witches' cold hands.

The thought made her double over. Her hands slammed on the frozen soil as she gasped for breath. She choked on her grief as if it were those same invisible hands strangling her.

"Selest!"

Thrion rushed to Selest's side completely unaware of the black figure rising behind him.

In her blurred vision, Selest saw a glint of steel cast in the faint gray light. Her heart caught in her throat.

With supernatural strength, she sprang to her feet and leaped between Thrion and his attacker.

It all happened so fast. She felt the dagger pierce through her, pain so cold, so numbing. She felt as if she were in a dream. It was a dream after all, was it not? She was no longer sure.

Thrion didn't have time to react before he saw the dagger plunging deep into her side.

She fell between them, writhing in agony.

Thrion was overcome with fiery rage.

He yelled in pure vengeance, sword raised as he spun in a tight circle.

With full force, he slew the foul villain.

The dagger fell from its grasp. The abysmal face screamed with fury at the heavens.

Thrion seized his chance. Quickly, he scooped the girl into his arms and sprinted across the path, fending off any Shadower within reach. Selest needed help from a healer. There was no time to waste.

"Faern!" Thrion shouted, panting heavily. Another Shadower upon a kelpie came from behind him. It closed the distance between them, poised to strike. He felt the pounding of the hooves vibrating against his chest.

The centaur fought off the remaining Shadowers astride their kelpies, jerking his head in Thrion's direction at the cry. As quick as lightning he unsheathed a dagger from behind him, aiming for the kelpie chasing him. He threw and it went zipping through the air in a great arc. Thrion saw it coming and swerved to the left just as the dagger struck the kelpie's eye, piercing through its skull.

It reared, screaming in pain, throwing off its rider. Those remaining charged the travelers from all directions.

Faern galloped toward the one nearest, and swung his sword and body like a mighty pendulum, knocking the beast off its feet and slaying its rider.

Panting and dripping with sweat and blood, he looked at the fallen figure of the girl. Blood drenched the right side of her dress where the dagger had made its mark.

"We need to seek help!" Thrion said.

"Give the child to me and get on!" Faern shouted. "Quickly!"

Thrion reached the centaur and handed him pain-stricken Selest. He swung onto the centaur's bloodied back.

Thrion noticed Faern bore a deep gash that ran from his chest to his back and saw the pain in the centaur's eyes.

Faern galloped along the road at great speed, their pursuers not far behind. Selest heard the galloping of hooves as a distant echo far, far away.

A numbness overcame her. The bite of ice gradually crept from her side, through her soul, seeping throughout her whole being, until it reached her heart.

She threw her head back against the centaur and became engulfed in pure suffering.

A terrible wail of pain escaped her lips. She cried out in agony for her mother and brother buried in the cold earth of The Glade taken from them by witches who murdered her father. She cried out for Wraith now in the Shadowers' grasp.

"AAAAAAAAHHHH!"

"AGGGGGGGGGGGGHHHHHHHHH!"

Those screams could not be her own. She felt something within her that was not her—as though she were possessed.

The same cold feeling she read of long ago in a poem. Only fragments could she recall in the fog of her consciousness.

> *...same cold breeze*
> *...rustles...leaves*
> *Blows...an icy gale*
> *Spirits...soaring...free*
> *Beyond...what...we...see...*

Reality struck her like lightning that foreshadows a storm.
A dagger of Emberthel made its mark on her body and soul.

Chapter 6

Selest's cries drowned out all other sources of sound. The trio fled for their only means of refuge, their pursuers closing in.

The brown specks of houses were like bison on the horizon.

"Looks about four miles hence," Thrion shouted to Faern.

The centaur breathed heavily.

Thrion felt dampness against his leg. He looked down and noticed the centaur's wound bleeding heavily. The cut from his back to his chest was very deep.

"Faern, were you cut by Emberthel?"

The centaur didn't answer. "Is—the church—close?" he wheezed.

Thrion's heart sank. "Faern—"

"Answer me!" Faern roared.

"Yes," he whispered, "but not you too."

When they reached the borders of the quiet little town, Faern stumbled to a halt.

Thrion slid off the centaur's bloody hide. Faern held the girl tight, as though she were the last innocent soul in all the realm.

Thrion tore a piece of tunic and wrapped it about the centaur's wounded chest. He repeated this task with Selest. She whimpered in pain.

Thrion avoided the girl's eyes. "Come," he whispered. "That should suffice for now."

He stumbled the remainder of the way, staggering as he pulled Selest from the centaur's weary arms into his own.

"We need—to reach—Father Zyon."

Thrion deciphered a horizontal line of deciduous trees. Their branches were nearly barren of fruit, yet a few red blossoms were still attached.

The leaves that had fallen formed a crimson carpet at their feet. It was as if the branches with menacing yet welcoming arms pulled them to certain doom.

The wind stirred the blossoms so they spiraled all about them; a faint cry caught up on the same breeze. It sliced through them like a knife; a hiss like vapors of steam from a great fire.

They staggered down the eerily beautiful yet morbid path and into the desolate village.

Selest was numb. She didn't know whether she was dead or alive.

With some strength she forced her eyes to open ever so slightly. She saw the blurred faces of Thrion and Faern growing more distant each time as if she were slipping away.

"Hold on, Selest, just a little longer," an echo of a voice said to her.

Just a little longer.

They hastened for the steeple with all the strength they could muster.

The church bell rang. The sound of a horn followed. The three short blows would warn the whole village. But it would not stop their pursuers from going in for the kill.

They stumbled on a cobbled road lined by an array of spruce cabins. Soon it gave way to a courtyard.

In the center was a circular fountain carved of granite, the water frozen in mid-spray.

Not a soul stirred. A lonely aura blanketed the village.

Cries of their pursuers grew louder.

"We're near the church," Thrion yelled over the howling wind. He led the centaur north of the courtyard.

Lower and lower the snow clouds descended on the weary travelers.

A great shadow soon engulfed them. They rushed up the steps of the church. Thrion pounded frantically with the ring attached to a heavily bolted door.

After a long moment of silence, he heard shuffling at the door.

It creaked open. Orange light flooded them with warmth.

The light revealed a stout old dwarf. "Who are ye?" he asked in a gruff voice.

"Thrion son of Yaelas. My companions and I have come in need of dire aid. Father Zyon is expecting us."

His dull eyes lit with recognition. He turned, yelling, "Have one of the lads call for the Father. He has company." The dwarf opened the door further and gestured for them to enter.

After a long moment, a bent figure clothed in a red robe appeared. A silver chain adorned his neck; at the center gleamed a seven-pointed star bejeweled with seven diamonds at the tips. A sapphire dominated the center.

"Father Zyon, please, we need your aid. My friends are injured."

The priest's blue eyes peered at their wounded states. "Thrion, come hither. I was expecting you."

The priest shut the door quickly behind them. "This way," he said. He led them down a vast, stone hallway illuminated by warm lamplight.

"Is this church fortified enough to keep out eleven Shadowers?" asked Faern as they walked along the blood-red carpet that lay before them, giving way to a sanctuary.

"Not one hath been able to break thro' these doors, not even since the

Glacian King waged war on the Snowess herself," said the priest with pride.

On either side, pews stretched far and wide. Within those pews were many dwarves that appeared to be wounded or pale with grief.

Before them, a pulpit stood at the front, but what took their breath away was the stained glass window. Dim sunlight peeked through the storm's thick veil, animating a sketch of a seven-pointed star, white in color. The glass outlining the star gleamed a deep blue.

Zyon called to someone at the nearest pew. "We needeth a healer, please, come forth. We art in dire need of aid."

A pale-skinned dwarf appeared. His hair and beard were a dark brown, and his eyes an icy blue. Under his fur-trimmed cape, he wore a leather tunic and leather pants. Zyon addressed him warmly.

"Ah, Adair, dear friend. We art in need of thine assistance." The priest turned to them. "'Tis Adair son of Aiden of Carahadrim. He is well known amongst his people as their Chief Healer."

The dwarf bowed his head in greeting. "Ye called, Father?"

"Refugees from the West hath come into our care. Please attendeth to their wounds."

Adair furrowed his brow, looking at Selest and Faern in turn.

"What befell ye?"

Thrion's gaze faltered. "We were ambushed by Shadowers. They were wounded by Emberthel blades."

Zyon's expression was grave. "This way." The priest led them east of the sanctuary into a dimly lit room. A table strewn with an array of parchments and the Eternal Book sat facing a cold hearth.

"Father, clear the table, an' fetch me some kindling," said Adair.

As Zyon did so, he turned to Thrion. "Lay her on the table."

Thrion settled Selest gently while Adair withdrew his satchel and retrieved an assortment of herbs.

As Zyon returned with the fuel, he lit the fireplace with a match. The hearth came to life filling the room with warmth. The bright flame cast an orange aura upon the girl's pale face. Zyon said a prayer over her.

Adair peered at Thrion. "You. Fetch me some water to clean her wound."

Zyon, poking at the fire, turned to Thrion and said, "Go into the sanctuary, Thrion. There is a bowl on the altar top on the platform. Then behind the pulpit, there is a store of water thou might collect."

Thrion dashed for the altar cabinet and grabbed a simple bowl used for offerings. Then he went to the entrance and retrieved water from a stoup. He returned to the small room and placed the water over the hearth.

"How long ago was it when the wounds were inflicted?" Adair looked at the girl and centaur with deep concern.

"We were about four miles from here. One hour at the most," Thrion answered.

Faern settled beside Selest, laying one hand on her shoulder, the other clenching his chest wound.

Adair withdrew a small knife and cut Selest's dress, revealing the wound.

His expression was grave. "I'll do what I must." He soaked a cloth in boiling water and sprinkled it with vinegar. Wringing it out, he placed it upon the girl's cut.

Selest felt tendrils of rekindled pain shoot through her side. She screamed, thrashing violently.

"Hold her!" Adair commanded.

Faern locked her arms in place while Thrion gripped her legs.

She strained in their grasp, but they remained firm.

The dwarf's manner became more cautious. Never had Adair treated a girl, especially one so young.

A blanket of white hot pain scorched her side. The same pain shot into her breast. Selest gritted her teeth, writhing in a sea of searing agony.

Zyon whispered a prayer.

Slowly, a white blur obscured her vision as the pounding in her side intensified.

Adair concocted chamomile tea in a small tin cup and mixed it with strange herbs. A few moments later he gave it to the girl. "Drink this, little Raven. 'Twill help ease the pain." He supported her head as she sipped the drink. The taste was mellow and honey-like.

She relaxed. Faern and Thrion loosened their grip.

After Adair removed the warm rag, he fetched bandages from his satchel and began dressing her midsection.

Thrion found a pillow to place under her head to make her comfortable. Faern knelt at her side, taking both her hands in his. Selest peered into his brown eyes which were filled with relief.

Adair then turned his attention to the centaur.

Faern gritted his teeth, breathing through the pain. But the calming touch of the girl comforted him. "You are quite skilled in the art of healing, Master Dwarf."

"'Tis been my profession for o'er twenty years. But ne'er had I treated one as fair and resilient as she. Tell me, girl, what's yer name?"

"Selest of The Glade, sir," she breathed heavily.

"An' what of yer companions?"

"I'm Thrion, son of Yaelas of the Misty Forest."

"And I am Faern of Perisade. We were ambushed by agents of the Deceptor." He continued, "Now that the Cow-skull Witches have taken The Glade, they will only grow in number, and soon spread beyond the borders."

"Will they take Snowtown as well?" asked Selest, fear rising in her belly.

Adair bandaged Faern's wound. "Don't fear, little Raven. The cold climate here is their sole weakness, but they have, no doubt, spread along the Lone Road to the Emerald Dells."

Faern growled like a wolf snarling at its enemy. "Those dells, green and fair, will now succumb to a sickly gray." He mourned the loss of his home.

"Alas," Zyon continued in solidarity, "I fear the witches harrowing the dells wilt possibly form an alliance with the Shadowers if they hath not already."

"I wouldn't be surprised if the demons of Filiath have awoken," said Adair. "The mines of the Silver Mountains have been abandoned for thousands 'o years. The White Mountains whence I reside have been overrun by those very demons. 'Tis why myself and my people have sought refuge in the father's house. The demons have spread from the connected regions of Dwindloth to Carahadrim."

"Then we shall take back Westerland, and be rid of the evil that dwells therein," Faern declared.

Selest clenched her pocket as the pain slowly subsided.

She withdrew the Key and clutched it to her breast, like a corpse clinging to the last remnants of life.

Adair was the first to notice. "By Darragh!" At the dwarf's outburst, everyone's attention was directed at the Key; its ethereal beauty could not be ignored.

"How didst thou end up possessing this token of Heaven?" the priest asked in a hushed tone, pointing a trembling hand at the Key. "For that— that is the Key of Ezelex."

Selest hesitated. "M-my father gave it to me when the witches attacked. How he came to possess it, I know not."

Father Zyon retrieved a book from the mantel, settling in a chair beside Selest.

"Tell me, daughter, art thou familiar with the Key's origin?"

She winced. "Bits and pieces."

Zyon flipped through the silver-trimmed pages. "I will share with thee an account of the First Era of Deceiving. This took place after the Forging of the Key which was fashioned to lock the Devil and his rebels away. Asteral charged the twelve angelic guards, now the Shadowers, to safeguard the

Key." His expression grew grave. "Alas, many were swayed that day."

Selest relaxed, drifting into a time long passed.

It reminded her of Yuletide when she and her mother would sit around the fire while her father read from the Eternal Book.

Clearing his throat, Zyon opened the volume and read:

...A meeting of the Children of the Inner Realm was held. Each race sent a representative to Falendell, where the Key was guarded. They wanted to be their own people and saw the Devil as a hero after he rebelled against Heaven and was locked away in the land of Fhar. They thought if they freed him, they could form an alliance with him and overthrow Asteral with an army tenfold.

After many councils, they decided to travel to the plains of Falendell to confront the guards and convince them to use the Key to unlock the door, thus freeing the Devil from his tomb.

The angelic guard (the Twelve) also became tempted by the Children of the Inner Realm's influence.

Only one resisted. His name was Garren. He tried to stop the rebellion, but he was overpowered by Rofur, the first Kinslayer. His fallen brothers stole the Key and traveled to Fhar in hopes of unlocking the door and forming an alliance with the Devil to overthrow Asteral.

After passing through plains, navigating through the dark forest, and traveling through the Silver Mountains, they reached Fhar.

Immediately those who opposed the Tempted were alerted. Many tried to stop them. But their forces were too great to overcome; many gave in.

On that day, man's humility turned into pride, dwarves' generosity turned into greed, centaurs' wisdom turned into foolishness, and the fauns' diligence turned into laziness.

Perhaps the worst thing: Love turned into hate.

They sent one representative of each of their races to partake in unlocking the door. Rofur was chosen to complete the evil task.

As it opened, discord and chaos erupted. A storm broke out, and blood rained down.

Some say it was the tears of the Heavenly Host mourning over the carelessness of Asteral's Children. For it is said the host wanted to come down and put an end to this.

But Asteral held them back, telling them the End was not yet near.

The unlocked door unleashed many evil things. Alas, the rebels cried out in agony as they realized their error and tried to ward off the oncoming evil.

Then a voice rang from the skies, declaring:

"This was your doing, as you have given into the temptation that poisons

the heart.

"From this day, evil will now and forever rule your hearts, though there are some that may yet resist. But now, archangels, your rank will be declined, and no longer will you have the gift of flight. You are no longer welcome in the Eternal Sky to join your brothers, for you have also given into evil. And to my Children of Dust, Root, and Stone, all of you have succumbed to the angels' choices, and have sought them as higher rank, and have let them have the final say. To all of you, I give mortality, and the only way to the Eternal Sky is through the penalty of death, but there you can go if you are still faithful to me. But whoever does not repent will be banished to the Abysmal Deep.

"It is because of your doing that the portal between the Eternal Sky and the Inner Realm ceases to exist. It was all of you who hath made it rain blood, and it will continue to do so until a new Key Bearer comes forth on good accord and seals evil once more—unblinded by their own desire. Only then will the prophecy be fulfilled."

At that moment, Asteral set a prophecy written in the stars.

Zyon closed the book. "I have read this account to remind each of thee of the dangers of revealing the knowledge of the Key to others. Thou must keepeth it a secret. Be careful who you trust. Thou must findeth Yaelas once you have reached the Council. No one else must know. If they do, they will try to stop thee from sealing the door."

Selest peered at the stained glass. Moonlight filtered through the many shapes which, like a puzzle, fit together creating a portrait of life.

"You are only a fragment that portrays a beauty cold and isolated," Thrion murmured to himself. "One cannot be whole without being broken. That was how the dark crafts were spun from the hem of Evildoers: Weavers of the abysmal thread of lies and deceit."

Fulfill the good of the earth for in Asteral you shall be reborn...

As the snow began to blow, it whistled through the church's chimney shafts as the small gathering sat by the warm glow of the fire. Sparks popped and crackled.

Thrion's eyes never left the girl's pale face. He eyed the bandaged midsection, tears pooling in his eyes.

Sensing his agony, Zyon knelt beside him. "Despair not, brother, for in thy darkest hour there is yet a ray of hope."

Thrion raised his gaze, his eyes red and swollen. "Do not speak of hope to me when there is none!"

Zyon's gaze bore deep into the young man's eyes which were dark with determination. "I see in thine eyes a brave and fierce warrior who hath many trials. There is a loss in a part of thee that groweth darker each day, yearning to be free from the prison of despair."

"Forgive me—" Thrion cried. "It's just—she sacrificed herself for my sake."

Zyon smiled grimly. "'Tis the spirit of a true friend. I only pray to Asteral above she wilt findeth peace in His arms."

Thrion sobbed. "No, I cannot bear the thought of losing her. It would prove too cruel." He peered at Adair. "Is she…?" his voice trailed.

Adair folded his arms across his chest, staring at the constellations engraved on the wooden floor. "I've done all that I can, lad. Only Evenmint can save them now."

Silence enveloped the room. Even the wind ceased to blow.

"Where does it grow?" asked Thrion.

"It grows on evergreen trees in Twilforest."

"That is the realm of the Snowess," Faern said. "Do you know if she still dwells there?"

The dwarven healer looked at the centaur and the girl, his eyes filled with concern. "Don't tell me all of ye plan to travel; yer too wounded," his gaze rested on the girl. "The young lass, especially."

Thrion's tone was firm. "We have no time to waste. Faern and Selest are in dire need. They need the Evenmint as soon as possible, so they must make the journey."

Zyon peered at all of them. "Thou can but taketh the chance. Venture across the Glase Pass. There, retrieve the Evenmint. From there, seeketh refuge in the house of the Snowess. May Asteral watch o'er thee." He made a sign of blessing over them.

"We can travel under the blanket of the snow," Thrion said. "We are anxious to keep our whereabouts hidden from the Shadowers."

"I suggest waiting till early morn," said Zyon. "The journey is perilous and thou must preserveth thy strength."

"No. I am afraid," Selest wheezed. "I do not have the courage for such a task. I've already lost my father and almost lost Thrion. I don't want to lose anyone else I hold dear."

"Take heart, dear one," said Zyon. "Having courage doesn't mean we art not also afraid. 'Tis through our fear that we turneth to Asteral for courage. 'Tis what makes us brave."

Selest took the words to heart, though she was barely conscious.

"Thou wilt need a healer to attend to thy wounds," said Zyon, turning to Adair. "I believe it is Asteral's will for thee to accompany them, Adair, son of Aiden. Their destination is Orai. There, thou shalt act as a representative for the Snowy Region."

"But Father, my place is with my kin."

Zyon gave the dwarf a firm but understanding look. "'Tis not our will but Asteral's that governs our fates."

Adair bowed his head in obedience.

"I shall sayeth a prayer for you," the priest offered.

They formed a small ring, bowing their heads and shedding silent tears in remembrance of the ones they had lost, now in the Eternal Sky.

"I wish for thee to part with a gift." Zyon unclasped the necklace from his neck and gave it to Thrion.

"Show this to thy father. Let him know that thou hath reached my doors alive and as proof of thy peril if any may deem it a jest. Also," he added, "let it be a token of good faith."

Thrion graciously accepted the necklace and stuffed it in his tunic pocket.

"You are not coming?" he asked. "My father would be thrilled to see you at the Council."

Zyon bowed his head. "Dwarven refugees from the White Mountains needeth the church's aid; I wilt not abandon them in these dark hours. My place is here."

Thrion nodded. "Then we thank you from the bottom of our hearts."

The howling breeze haunted the inhabitants that night. Despite being wrapped in a woolen blanket, Selest felt the cold slice her skin.

She focused her gaze on the fire's entrancing glow wondering what lay ahead.

Asteral, where are You? Can You hear my cries of pain? Please, make it cease.

She glanced at the others. Faern was slumped against the wall, his chest bandaged. She wondered if he felt the same pain that she did. Maybe so. 'Twas likely he endured better than her, being a veteran of war and all, she mused.

Bouts of snoring interrupted her thoughts. She noticed the dwarf sleeping soundly by the fireside's corner.

But no sign of Thrion. She wanted to cry out, but she didn't want to disturb the others. She bit her tongue. If Faern could bear it, so could she.

But the pain proved too much. She pleaded, "Asteral please take this pain, please! I can't bear it!"

She squeezed her eyes shut. Quiet sobs wracked her body as she cried herself to sleep.

Chapter 7

The next morning after a quick breakfast they gathered supplies provided by the priest and exchanged their farewells.

Father Zyon blessed each one of them and pressed a small bag of coins in Thrion's hand. "On the northern edge of town, thou will findeth a livery with horses and possibly the food and supplies needeth for the journey. Go now, and may the comforting presence of Asteral be with us all."

Selest smiled, her heart full of longing. "Will we ever see you again, Father?"

"Be it under mortal stars or Heaven's light, that you shall."

Thrion bowed. "We thank you for your kind hospitality, Father. Yaelas will be pleased to hear of your well-being."

Zyon placed both hands on his shoulders. "And I of his. In the meantime, Asteral leadeth us on different paths."

Thrion held Selest, who was wrapped in a woolen blanket, close to his chest.

Adair stared at the floor, unmoving. Faern urged him forward. "Come Master Dwarf. We need your aid." He glanced at the priest.

"Thy people are in good hands," Zyon reassured Adair.

With that, they exited the sanctuary and walked back into the harsh world. The freezing air stung their flesh.

In spite of dawn's hour, the veil of night cloaked their eyes as the snow continued to blow.

The morning chill took Selest's breath away. She peered at the sky above. Instead of the stars shining in brilliance to where one felt the urge to touch them, they seemed cold and remote.

They trekked through the biting cold struggling in vain to see through the blinding snow. The farther they traveled, the more veiled the stars became.

The wind whipped mercilessly about them.

With every step Thrion took, Selest's side pounded a fiery tempo that sent her world spinning. All their surroundings blurred as they trekked on through the cobblestone streets; the houses stared at them with black sockets.

Behind them, a cry as lonely as the stars split the night. Selest dared to look back, but could only see endless darkness. However, she felt an unseen force; a nameless fear pressing down on her. She imagined she heard the sound of the thundering of the hooves of their pursuers.

Selest shivered. After a while, the houses gave way to the icy tundra before them. Selest squinted, certain she spotted the livery stable in the distance.

As they approached, Adair tried the latch, but it was frozen solid. The stout dwarf kicked the stable doors open.

The building was dimly lit by a single lantern hanging from a peg overhead. They noticed a hallway covered in hay, with stalls lining either side. Horses and ponies gave a questioning neigh, poking their heads from their stalls in curiosity.

Thrion settled Selest on the stable floor.

Adair went to the tack room. "Gather all ye need lads, but leave all that can be spared."

Faern knelt beside Selest, watching the entrance.

Selest followed his gaze. "D-do you think they'll find us?"

Faern's chest heaved a massive sigh. "'Tis only a matter of time. We need only be ready to face them."

"Is there no escape?" she asked.

Faern's keen eyes never left the darkness. "It doesn't matter where we go, child. Evil is always present. Whether in plain sight or hidden from us. That is why we must be ready to fight it."

Selest pondered his words as Thrion found a steed to his liking—a black mountain pony appearing sturdy in the legs, bred for the cold harsh Icelands, no doubt.

Thrion coaxed him as he fetched a saddle nearby. He began fastening the saddle and bridle into place with a good deal of clenching and buckling.

The pony stomped in impatience. Thrion paid no heed. "Easy boy, easy." He soothed the pony, stroking its mane.

Adair popped out of the tack room. "Come everyone. Thrion, bring that pony forth."

With Selest in Faern's arms, and Thrion leading the pony, they entered through the tack room and past another door into another.

Before them, they beheld a sleigh of carven spruce.

Faern placed her gently in the sleigh.

Thrion hitched the pony. Adair approached the trembling girl and wrapped her with furs from the tack room. "There. Do ye feel secure, lass?"

Selest gave a weak smile. "Yes, thank you."

Faern trotted toward them. "So far our course is unknown, and that is why I seek counsel from you, Adair. You know these lands far better than any of us here."

"Aye, these mountains are a danger to all who attempt the journey. The Pass of Glasefell will provide us with the safest passage. But we ought to make for the pass with great caution; the danger lies all around."

Adair came to the driver's seat with a whip in hand. Thrion settled beside Selest.

"What would be before us?" Selest asked in alarm.

"Demons," Adair whispered with strained effort, a look of fear and remorse in his eyes. "Come, let us leave this frozen wasteland."

The wind blew mercilessly as the small union rode swiftly across the snowy tundra.

Adair drove the sleigh with ease with Faern taking up the rear, watching with keen eyes for any suspicious activity.

The falling snow was both a blessing and a curse, obscuring any sight or scent that the enemy relied on in finding them.

Gray clouds swirled threateningly in their midst. Small flakes danced about them in a frozen twirl promising the blizzard that was closing in fast.

They could barely see a thing in the falling snow, but the dim gray shapes of the White Mountains loomed before them, swallowing the company in their vastness.

Selest shrank inward at the sight of the mountains growing larger. But she again straightened her frame in the confidence of coming this far. She prayed the worst was behind them.

Alas, this proved in vain. Barely an hour had slipped by before she felt like surrendering herself to the cold.

She was glad for the numb feeling for it dulled the pain, but it could not numb the dread of facing the great storm's wrath.

She simply held on knowing that with every journey where there was a beginning, there was also an end. And even if the end came with this stage of the Quest, she would be glad when it was over.

In the meantime, she took her mind off the sense of dread by letting her eyes wander across the vast range. Mountainous silhouettes were seen in black. Though she couldn't view them clearly, she could feel the mountains' claustrophobic presence.

Gazing out into nothingness, she felt a strong sensation of sadness. And then she saw it—a dark shadow, darker than the shades surrounding it. She guessed it correctly to be Adair's home in the White Mountains.

She glanced over at him and was sure she saw the slightest movement of Adair looking out in the same direction. Fresh tendrils of grief stung at her heart drawn to his heartache. Then he turned away, head bowed in remembrance of the fallen who had perished at the hands of the demons.

Dark shapes morphed in the white. Selest screamed, fearing her fantasies were coming to life.

The Shadower reared upon its steed, blade raised.

Faern drew his sword. "Run!"

Adair prompted the steed to a gallop.

As the wind sliced through their clothing, Selest huddled deeper into her coat with her eyes closed to shut out the horror around her and turned into Thrion's furs, shielding her face from the penetrating cold.

They moved east along the looming range and crossed to the Pass of Glasefell.

The pony struggled to maintain its pace as they made the lofty ascent.

"They're getting closer!" yelled Thrion.

The leader of the Eleven advanced.

Selest dared a glance from the steep pass. The town grew smaller and smaller until it was engulfed by the swirling snow. Her life flashed before her eyes. She envisioned herself falling into a bottomless pit, being torn limb from limb by the snatching hands of the Shadowers, screaming for help, the cry going unanswered.

A dull flash caught her eye.

"Faern!" she yelled. The Shadower gave a mighty blow. The pass was too narrow—the centaur was trapped.

Thrion fumbled with his quiver of arrows. His fingers were stone-cold, making the task difficult.

The Shadower slashed at his hide. Faern cried out to the heavens, his plea mingled with the howling torrent above.

With the last of his strength, he gave a swift kick at the Shadower's mount. The kelpie stumbled in the snow.

Thrion aimed above the enemy. Letting loose his arrow, it made its unseen mark.

A tremor shook through the entire mountain. Selest thought the sleigh would tip off the path and into the white nothingness below. She screamed, holding on for dear life as a river of white cascaded down the hillside above them.

Adair urged the horse into a full gallop.

Eyes wide, Selest cried out in desperation as Faern struggled to catch up. With a mighty leap, the centaur vaulted into the sleigh as the avalanche passed a hair's breadth behind them.

The sleigh came to a screeching halt.

The wind sliced like swords at their skin, freezing their blood to ice.

Selest clutched her side as it pounded in sync with her beating heart, eyes wide. "Faern?"

Thrion was at the centaur's side, shaking him. "Faern, can you hear me?"

He grunted. Thrion's brow furrowed with concern. "Can you stand?"

Faern strained under the pain of his wounds. The centaur sheathed his sword and stumbled forward.

"Come. We mustn't falter." Faern placed one leg in front of the other, gritting his teeth.

"Faern, you're too injured," Thrion said.

"Enough of me. I will endure for the girl's sake."

Tears ran down her face.

Faern and Thrion trudged through the ankle-deep snow that served as their trail.

Selest's heart went out to the centaur. Here she was in this sleigh, safe and secure, while the centaur had to brave the mountain's wrath on foot.

They continued making their way through with the winds whistling a merciless lament.

As they traversed the steep, narrow path, Adair warned, "It's slick with ice, lads. Take care!" His voice was distant and muffled in their numb ears.

And indeed it was. Not only that, but the snow fell as heavily as ever, blinding them to where all they could make out was a blank whiteness.

Selest felt as though she floated in a colorless dream. It was just the cold, that's all, she thought to herself.

Just—the cold—all sources of sound faded away. The whiteness about her blurred. All turned to nothingness.

Chapter 8

Darkness enshrouded them. Darkness so tangible, Selest thought if she reached out, she could feel its physical form.

Pinholes of crystalized drops formed. The crystals gleamed as clear as window panes. Within those tiny windows, they caught glimpses of a snowy white haven dotted with evergreens. Finally, the sun dawned fair and bright upon the frozen land.

The farther they traveled, the closer to reality the image seemed.

All they could do was continue to strain forward. All their other senses were smothered. The silence was surreal as a dream. The snowdrops cascading upon the void seemed to grow ever closer.

It was as if one peered at their reflection in a pond, leaning in so close to the surface only to fall headfirst underwater. The enchantment soon became reality. The veil lifted, and they found themselves once more on the mountain pass. All senses slowly returned. They took quick gulps of stinging air.

Thrion took in his surroundings. "What kind of sorcery did we come through?"

Adair fumbled with the reins. "This is unknown to me. I do not know what came to pass, but I know this: we have risen out of the veil and have passed the frozen wastelands."

Thrion shielded his eyes from the sun. "Where do you figure we are now?"

The very trees they foresaw in the droplets peeked from the arms of the snowy mountain. Their emerald berries gleamed like jewels amidst the soft blankets of crystal snow, and the air seemed to be glazed in iridescent silver light.

The forest was welcoming as they walked along the path outlined by holly trees. "I reckon we are in the heart of Twilforest," Adair said, eyeing the enchanting path. "But of Evenmint I see naught. Look for a stream. 'Tis where the herb grows."

As they continued on, they scanned through the trees searching for a stream.

Selest stared up in complete wonder. These trees were huge—larger than the row of pines in The Glade.

Suddenly, a faint movement stirred beyond them.

Thrion was the first to hear it. With a hunter's instinct, he unsheathed his sword. The others did the same.

A frozen silence hung in the air.

A white flash split the stillness with a mighty *whoosh!*

The quicksilver gust slowly morphed into a brilliant shimmering silhouette against the pale sun in the crystal clear blue sky. They made out the form of a deer; no, a stag. It landed soundlessly upon the glimmering snow. The beast's coat gleamed pure white. Its dark eyes peered at the newcomers.

Adair urged the pony onward. "Stay your weapons, lads. It's just a stag. We must find Evenmint," he glanced at the pale girl, "before it's too late."

At this, the stag's ears perked up. The beast turned. With one glance back, it bounded away.

"I think it wants us to follow him," Thrion said.

"Don't be daft. It's just some beast we frightened off," Adair scoffed.

"Adair, maybe Thrion's right," said Selest. One glance at the look in the girl's eyes, and the dwarf reluctantly agreed.

Adair urged the sled after the stag, with Faern and Thrion slowly stumbling after them.

They twisted and turned through a labyrinth of evergreens trying to keep up with the graceful waltz of the stag. The trees surrounding them were a silvery green blur.

The stag finally came to an effortless halt after what seemed a mile. The others slowed to a staggering walk. The pony heaved laboriously. The gulps of cold air stung their lungs. Before them where the stag stood was a clearing.

The trees formed a perfect ring, and in the middle of it lay a vast frozen lake. It reflected the pale clear blue sky that was laced with puffy white clouds. They peered at the sight in wonder for it seemed as though the sky was mirrored within itself. On the other side, they saw a perfect line of birch trees. Their slender branches were intertwined into an arc. Many beads of ice drops sewn into the wood twinkled like stars in the day. They seemed to shimmer before the entrance.

And around the pond grew a plethora of green plants—Evenmint!

Adair rushed over to the pond and plucked a handful of the ruby berries from the plant.

He withdrew a mortar and pestle from his satchel, and placed the red treasures within the container, crushing the berries. He then applied it to Selest's and Faern's wounds.

After Adair dressed their wounds with fresh bandages, the curtains of ice rustled.

They jerked their heads in that direction. Before them, a slender shadow behind the curtain emerged revealing a woman.

The woman's skin was as pale as evening-lit snow, yet her cheeks were red as though bitten by frost. She wore silky white robes etched in silver; a circlet of silver bejeweled with diamond snowflakes crowned her long silver hair. Her silver-pink eyes shone regally.

Thrion inched forward. "A-are you Crysil, the Snowess of this fair realm?"

"I am. And who are you to enter my domain?"

Thrion bowed. "My lady, we seek refuge. We have faced many perils and desire your hospitality."

She peered past his shoulder. "I can see that. What befell you?"

He bowed his head. "Shadowers wielded blades of Emberthel and injured my companions."

Crysil turned to the stag. "Ixilion, lead the guests on." She motioned across the pond and the stag bounded forward. He did not slip or lose his balance.

Faern and Thrion followed. Adair hesitated to pull the sleigh from the pond's edge.

Sensing his uneasiness, Crysil reassured him. "Do not be afraid. It provides safe passage unless I deem otherwise."

"How comforting," muttered Adair under his beard. Reluctantly, he urged the pony onward.

To Selest's surprise, the pond was clear as glass. So clear, she thought she would fall into her reflection.

As they followed the Virtue, Selest noticed the dwarf had his head bowed. "A-Adair, are you all right?"

He gave a start. "Aye, I'm fine. Just—" he glanced from whence they came, "looking behind."

Selest's heart ached for the dwarf. How awful it must be to leave behind your kin for the sake of a stranger's health. He had already had his own wounded brethren to look after.

"You miss them, don't you."

"Ye mean my lads? I do, lass. I guess I'm just not ready to leave behind the old and welcome the new. Yet," his voice trailed, "everything here seems frozen in time."

His world warped in and out, in and out, to an unnatural pulse.

Beneath the glassy facade, he saw mines. A pit with no end.

And he was falling.

Demons' cried deep all around, above and under—until the pony's hooves crunched on snow.

"Adair?" Selest placed a comforting hand on his shoulder. "I'm sorry you had to leave them behind. They were your kin and—"

"It's all right, Raven. I miss them. But the Father an' them can look after each other." He squeezed her hand reassuringly before pulling on the reins and halting the pony in place.

The Snowess peered at him with a knowing gaze. Their eyes locked for a moment. It was as though he were under some spell.

He stopped the pony and stumbled from the sleigh, gasping for air.

Everyone's eyes felt like icy needles pricking through his skin and into the most vulnerable part of him: the heart.

"Don't look at me in such a way. 'Tis unbearable; ye do not know my fear. My kin perished in the mines, their loss is a heavy weight I carry. Every breath, every heartbeat—lost—yet still living in my mind."

Crysil's feet crunched in the snow, approaching him. "Let your heart pour out for the broken, the lost, but the night will pass on into dawn, till all evil is gone."

He peered up at the Virtue, her wings spread around him in comfort.

She offered him a hand. "The pond reveals many reflections of oneself. Some are associated with our past, others are countless possibilities of what could be."

Adair hesitated at her words. Humiliation sprouted in his belly.

Without warning, Crysil took his hand. Her touch numbed him to the bone.

Adair withdrew like he had been bitten. He pulled away from her and returned to the sleigh, urging the pony forward. "Ye best lead on, Miss. My friends are wounded and they need to rest."

Crysil sighed. "Very well. Come. I shall lead you to the stables. There, you can tend to your steed."

As they continued on, Adair felt her cold gaze pierce through his skin.

Chapter 9

The pain in Selest's side dwindled, but the ache was still unbearable. She felt as though she were in a black pool of water. One moment she was drowning in inaudible words, the next she was above the surface, but the words still sounded distant.

"Come, I shall provide all that I can for the wounded," a silvery voice echoed.

"Your concern is much appreciated. Thank you for your hospitality," said Thrion.

"Yes, I echo that sentiment," Faern added.

Selest remained stone-still, stunned by the Virtue. In all the stories she had read, this angelic maiden reminded her of the one she heard in a poem long ago when she was living in a small cottage surrounded by pines.

"Ixilion, prepare the house. Tonight we are expecting guests." Bowing his mighty head, Ixilion turned and leaped straight away from view.

Crysil led them through the path shaped by the white birch. The trees glittered crystalline in the pale evening sun. And even in the eve's light, her wings gleamed all the more, a beacon in the snowy land.

"Forgive my questioning, but does your fortress provide enough protection from the Shadowers? They may be pursuing us as we speak," Thrion said.

"Nay, nothing comes through the Passage of Glasefell unless I am aware. Fear not, brave warrior, for here you are safe."

With that, Faern walked behind her, followed by Thrion, Selest, and Adair in the sleigh taking the rear. His head was still bowed in grief.

All was quiet for a moment, and then the snow angel spoke. "As was foretold in Legend, I am Crysil, HighSeer of the North; Snowess of the Graying, and the keeper of the Mirror."

It's just like in the stories. Selest thought. *Just like the stories...* And with that, she passed out.

Selest slowly gained consciousness as she opened her eyes. She felt a comforting weight over her. She noticed she was in a bed in a small room.

She felt an ache on her side pulsing to a peculiar beat.

One-two-three, One-two-three, One-two-three... She shook her head. She desired to be rid of the relentless tempo.

Peering out the window to take her mind off of the ache, she saw the rising pale sun peeking through the lattice. To her right she saw the mountain, its feet crowned with firs that appeared as silhouetted sentinels.

Crystals of ice chimed melodiously overhead.

Selest yawned and stretched. She felt her side; her entire midsection was freshly bandaged. She was also wearing an unfamiliar gown.

She reached into the pocket of the gown, gasping when she found it empty.

The Key.

She grasped at the other pocket more frantically. It was also empty. She grew pale.

Quickly, she got up from the bed, the sudden movement making her feel lightheaded. She barely made it to the door and had to support her thin frame on the knob. Once she regained her composure she opened the door, revealing a spacious domain. White trees were strewn as walls. Silver sconces hung overhead bearing white-wax candles giving off a soft orange glow. The light offered plenty of warmth from the biting tendrils of the North.

The floor was white marble. A white oaken table and chairs stood at the center.

Seated at the table were her companions. However, it was the pale-winged woman that held her attention. She had heard only fragments of what had occurred since the stag crossed their path.

They all jumped up at the sight of her.

"Selest—"

Thrion rushed out of his seat.

She grabbed him by the shoulders, nearly hysterical. She leaned in close, startling him all the more. "The Key," she dared whisper, "where—?"

He patted his breast pocket. Relief flooded over her. "How is your wound?" he asked.

"It just aches, almost like a pulse."

"Let me see, child." Crysil rose from her seat and in a few graceful steps was towering before her.

She stood above Selest, wings folded, shining in the orange candlelight.

Selest looked up and peered into her silver-pink eyes filled with the wisdom of many snowy dawns.

Putting both hands on the thin girl's shoulders, Crysil began to guide her to a side room.

Almost instinctively Adair snatched his satchel.

Crysil noticed. "There will be no need for that, Master Dwarf. Once I take a good look at her, she will be just fine."

Adair rose from his seat. "With all due respect, Milady, it is my occupation to assist the hurt—"

"I am afraid your skills in medicine won't be of any use, Master Adair. If my prognosis is correct, then she requires my urgent attention."

Adair looked at the young girl. She hesitated. "Selest, are you comfortable with this?"

"I'd rather not."

For a brief moment, she swore she caught a glimpse of magenta shooting through Crysil's eyes.

"You have been having dizzy spells frequently, have you not?" the Virtue asked as Selest's heart quickened.

"Y-yes—" the color drained from her face, "how do you know?"

"You are eighteen, no?"

"I—I turned seventeen merely a month or so ago."

"Ah, I see, a late bloomer, but a good age nonetheless."

Selest blushed.

Thrion stared hard at the Gray Virtue. "Milady, what are you trying to say?"

"So you do not know what it means then?" She furrowed her brow. Crysil's eyes were filled with questions. Selest grew impatient.

Crysil bit her bottom lip, considering.

Finally, she spoke, "Your wings have begun to grow."

Selest stared at the marble floor and laughed nervously.

"With all due respect, Snowess, but I hail from The Glade. Only simple archangels once resided there."

"Oh come now, everyone knows ever since the Third Era that archangels and angelic monks have always resided in The Glade."

"Yes, but they were killed off. Only angels and humans remained. So it's impossible to say that I am an—archangel."

Bile rose in her throat, causing her to choke.

Crysil furrowed her brow. "Wasn't one of your parents an archangel? Did they not tell you?"

"No, they're dead." Selest grew irritated.

"I am deeply sorry to hear that, child. But do you not know of your ancestry?"

"Yes, I do. The first peoples of The Glade were archangelic prophets, and they were given wings unique to the other archangels, for they were prophets sent by Asteral himself. But that was a very long time ago. Archangels dwell there no more. The last one ever accounted for was Elarael, who was slain by a witch."

Crysil straightened. "And do you know what happened?"

Selest lowered her gaze to the floor. "I…"

"After Elarael, wife to the Virtue Autumn, was slain because of her wings, other archangels began to cut off their wings during the Siege of the West."

"Yes, but—"

"After they cut their wings, they continued the same tradition thereafter, and to their offspring, depending on when they received their wings."

"If what you say is true, then why didn't my parents warn me?" Selest asked angrily.

"Your wings bloomed late. This knowledge was probably unknown to them. And if they did know, they would've told you of this perilous fate. I deem your wings have taken full root and will sprout to their full length over time."

"W-when will they reach their full stage?" Selest said, her vision blurring into a silent ocean of tears.

"Within a week's time the wings will split the skin and begin to grow. But," she strode to her side, "if I examine them, I'll know exactly what stage they are at."

Selest said nothing. The slight weight on her back proved the truth of the revelation.

She sighed, raising her gaze. "A-all right. I guess it's most appropriate if you do so, with you having wings and all, but—" she said hesitantly, looking at Adair.

"I'd feel more comfortable if Adair were there to assist me," Crysil quickly added, "and I am sure he would gain much insight so as to treat winged folk in the future."

Crysil stared at the dwarf, who immediately gathered his medical supplies.

"Are you certain of this?" he asked Selest.

"Yes."

"Very well."

Crysil led them into a corner room. When they entered through a white door, she saw that a bed stood in the middle. It was covered in white fox pelts and stood near a roaring hearth. An orange fire cast the room in dark peach shadows.

Crysil directed Selest to a bed.

Selest's thoughts twisted her surroundings. They warped in and out, near and far. In and out, in and out.

The Virtue glided across the room, footsteps light as snowfall. Selest's vision blurred in her state of surreality.

Crysil returned with a silken raven-blue garment that shimmered in the dawning sunlight. "This clothing is designed specifically for winged folk. It will give your wings plenty of room to sprout."

Selest accepted the dress and went behind a white partition to change.

Cautiously, she slipped the garment about her. It hugged her form lavishly.

When she turned, looking in the mirror, her eyes widened. Two identical lumps had formed on her back. She then noticed a tiny wing trying to develop. She started shaking uncontrollably.

"Why did they keep this from me?" she rasped. Coming from behind the partition, she settled herself on a chair.

Crysil approached her and placed two hands on her upper back. Her touch was like ice—cold and hard. She gasped as the pain began to bloom throughout her back to her chest.

Adair rushed forward. "Let me examine her wings. She needs a gentle touch—"

Crysil sighed. "The pain is only normal."

"Adair—" Selest blurted. "Let him examine them, please. Your touch is numbing. I cannot bear it."

Adair nodded. "Aye, she needs heat. If her wings have been forming for a while it will help her muscles relax."

The sudden panic welling up inside her subsided.

Crysil's eye twitched, but she quickly regained her composure. "Very well. Dinner is ready for you, whenever you're ready for it. Is there anything else I can do for you?"

"No. Thank ye for yer concern," Adair said. The Snowess turned and closed the door softly behind her.

Adair rose. "I'm going to fetch a bowl of water. For now, rest."

When he left, Selest couldn't help but trace the lumps on her back. Pain shot up her neck to her skull and pulsed in the depths of her brain. A thin red line clouded her vision.

She fell to the bed and gritted her teeth. She had a white-knuckled grip on the fox's pelt. She writhed in pain that felt like a red-hot flame. This pain was much different and much worse than the cut wound. She squeezed her eyes shut and hid away within a world of starlit holidays, angelic poems, and The Glade.

The door behind her opened.

Selest recognized the heavy footsteps of the dwarf. He drenched a rag in a bowl of hot water and rubbed Selest's back.

The dwarf broke out in song, in hopes to soothe the girl. He recalled the songs the minstrels would always sing in the dwarven halls.

Beneath Silver Mountain,
Runs a jeweled fountain.
In the rush of a river, poverty will deliver,

O'er the lunar eye of the mountain.

Engraved in shade is the jagged peak,
Upon winter's snowdrops bleak.
As dwarves trudge through the snow, to and fro,
Shelter from the raging storm they seek.

Lost they were in biting cold,
In the mourning pines of old.
As roaring thunder shakes frozen under,
Cast by the moon, a phantom veil of despair hence unfolds.

Below the starry sleeves,
Ageless within many eves.
The dwarves there dwelt, ere the winter's melt,
Carried on the cool summit breeze.

Oh, on that clear and crisp lone night,
The moon gleamed in crystal light.
In pools of nightshade, as stars fade,
The wildlands were showered in white.

They deem this as a sign,
Seven stars remain aligned.
In the dimming light crowned was the height,
A prophecy created by the Divine.

Before the doorstep, a door was cast by a ray of a star,
Mirrored upon the entrance seen from afar.
They hastened into the vast hall beyond the gray-stoned wall,
Near the reflected door latched by an enchanted bar.

Oh! The king has come unto his kin,
Under the mantle of snow therein.
Foreshadows thawing leaf, laying in the sheaf,
And so they must be away within.

As the mighty lord took up his throne,
Of ancient carven stone.
Wrought from mines they sought,

He came to his own.

Fashioned was he of silver chain,
Matched by an iron sword wielded by a bloody stain.
A cape he wore, of a hide a white stag once bore,
From the iron spurs to the silver height, in utter surety, he
shall reign…

Long years passed, as the dwarves mined for white and clear gems,
Beneath the graying peak dim.
In the deep, where demons sleep,
With torches blazing fiery and grim.

Uncovering Hell's darkened womb,
The dwarves met their doom.
With iron picks and shovels, they dug brick by brick,
Only for the mines to be their very tomb.

Beneath Silver Mountain, runs an ashed fountain,
In the rush of the river, poverty shall no longer deliver.
O'er the lunar eye of the mountain,
Runs an ashen fountain.

Ever they delved deeper within,
Awakening the dead who slaughtered their kin.
A people who lived valiantly, and who fought gallantly,
Met their doom lying therein.

Selest stared into the flames entranced by the mournful tone. For a moment all her pain was forgotten.

Sunlight filtered through the windows washing over Selest like a welcoming embrace.

"How do they feel?"

"They just feel—odd."

"Aye, yer wings have taken root and will take a week to sprout, Raven. 'Tis normal for them to feel a bit out of place," he reassured her. "The muscles are healthy, but yer bones are still fragile. I would be careful if I were you. Ye've yet to grow into them, and are therefore not yet strong."

"I still can't believe my parents kept this from me." She quickly added,

"You know, I am thankful for what Asteral has made me, but the past still remains unclear."

"'Tis part of this world, the unclearness of things. We must place our trust in Asteral to make the way clear." Adair motioned to the door. "Come, 'twill speed the healing if ye don't lie abed all day."

Together, they exited the room. The scent of baked goose and sweet berries wafted through the room. Laughter rang throughout the rafters.

As they approached the dining hall, a merry dinner welcomed them. Upon the table, candles flickered in and out almost hypnotically. Rainbows danced about the silver platters and the crystal ware.

The Virtue greeted them with a radiant glow of hospitality.

"Are your new wings faring better?" she asked.

"I suppose," Selest said as Crysil pulled her to a chair. Selest marveled at the scrumptious sight before her. The table was abundant with roasted duck, fried goose, cooked stag, fried cabbage, rabbit stew, nuts, butterscotch pudding, and the most appetizing oat bread she had ever seen. She spotted a bowl of ruby-red apples and gooseberries and mulled wine—reminders of home.

"Come now child, please help yourself to some nourishment."

She shook her head. "Nay, I am not hungry. Forgive me, my lady, but I'm still trying to get over the day's events."

"Oh, come now Selest, eat your fill and drink your worries away!" It was Thrion's voice—merry as a loon.

Selest started. The composure that was a constant in Thrion's eyes was replaced with uncontrollable gaiety. He held a cup of wine in the air. "Cheers, my fine centaur."

Hic! "Cheers, my fine man!" The calm and observant centaur was now so inattentive that he did not once acknowledge their presence. Thrion slammed so hard on the table that the crystal ware nearly toppled to the floor.

Selest peered at the food once more. Her mouth watered.

"Thrion, Faern, what in the blazes has gotten into ye?" exclaimed Adair. The two jovial men paid little heed.

"Lads, get a hold of yerselves," Adair said, clasping them both on the shoulders. He peered at Faern's wound. "Especially you, centaur, all this wine could prove ill for yer wound."

Faern dismissed the dwarf. "Come, drink, and get to know me better. 'Tis a cheerful time!"

"What in the blazes has gotten into ye?" Adair yelled again. "Tisn't like ye to jest about in such dire circumstances."

Crysil broke into merry laughter. "Oh, come now Master Dwarf. Do be of good tidings."

Adair rose. "I ought to change the dressing on the girl's wounds. Her health is in my care after all."

He nodded at Selest, who was about to help herself to some gooseberry pie. "C'mon lass, best not be long."

Before Selest could protest, the dwarf took her hand and led her back to her room, shutting the door behind them.

"Adair, what in Asteral's name has gotten into you? I'm starving, why are you—"

He raised a finger to his lips. Adair led her to the corner of the room where he could be sure no one was listening.

"Something doesn't feel right, lass. Your friends have acted quite odd after they sat down to feast."

"Do you think she poisoned the food?" Selest asked.

"No doubt. Cast a spell to make the poison more effective maybe."

"All the tales I've read about her recalled her as a hero. When she reclaimed her son's throne after the Winter War, she pledged peace," Selest reasoned.

Adair thought of this. "My kin traded gems of star sapphire to her in exchange for Evenmint. 'Tis the only connection we have with her."

"But that doesn't—"

"Ne'er did she offer us sanctuary when the Demons of Filiath took our home," he hissed. "I know my people grasped too greedily for those gems because it was their birthright. Those of us that survived were lucky to make it out alive."

Selest placed a hand on his shoulder. "I'm sorry, Adair. What are you trying to conclude about Crysil?"

"I think for whatever reason she's trying to kill us."

Selest reeled back. "But why?"

"She's a traitor to her kind. Just like her own son," Adair said. "She reclaimed his throne to reign even more powerful."

"But she had promised peace—"

"She declared peace as a means of remaining neutral," he explained. "It's only a ruse to gain more power."

"How do we break the spell?"

Adair fingered the hilt of his dagger. "I—I don't know, lass." He looked her hard in the eye. "Whatever ye do, don't eat or drink her fare."

Selest felt all the color drain from her face. "I won't. But what about Faern and Thrion? It seems the more they consume the more they're trapped in their fantasies."

Adair sighed. "We should flee this place." He eyed the girl, eyes full of concern. "But ye aren't well. Ye still need to recover from yer stab wound, not to mention adjusting to yer wings."

"But the others—"

"I'll handle it. Ye need to recover." Adair gave her one final, stern look.

"Adair—" She glanced at the door, pale with fright.

She knelt at the dwarf's level. Her entire body shook as she placed her slender hands on the dwarf's shoulders. Quiet as a mouse, she whispered, "The Key. Thrion has the Key. Ever since I passed out he has held onto it for safekeeping."

Adair's eyes widened. "Ye don't have it?"

She shook her head. "If she gets her hands on it—"

Adair turned for the door. "I-I'll take care of it, lass. Ye rest."

Before he left, he handed her some berries from his satchel. "Here. This should hold you over for now. Until then, don't eat the lady's food, lest ya end up like them."

Selest accepted the berries. "Please be careful."

"I will." Adair shut the door softly behind him. As he turned, he found the towering figure of the Virtue standing right in front of him. She smiled vibrantly at him. "Why do you hide away like a vanishing wisp? Come, you have waited long enough. Feast with us."

Adair turned to the others. "Aye, come and join us, we shall hearken back all night," chimed Faern in drunken gaiety.

"I shall have to pass," the dwarf replied.

He approached the two men. Thrion offered him a goose leg. "Let your spirits be filled with good tidings and cheer."

Adair slapped it out of his hand. He caught sight of Faern drinking a cup of wine and slapped that out of his hand as well. "Get hold of yerselves lads. Can ye not come to reason?"

"You—" Crysil gritted her teeth as Faern's cup continued to spin on the marble floor.

Adair remained rooted to the ground, unsheathing his dagger. "I know what ye did to my friends."

Her pupils dilated until her eyes were black as night. Before Adair could react, the woman charged. She convulsed, twisting in seemingly impossible angles. Blood poured out of her eyes and nose, followed by her mouth.

Adair stared in horror. "What—?"

Void tears streamed down the Virtue's cheeks. She burst into a frenzy and charged him.

Adair sliced her shoulder when she tried to advance closer.

She screeched with an unearthly cry.

"This was a trap!" yelled the dwarf.

A stench of an ancient corpse filled the air; tears began to sting his eyes.

Adair struck her, leaving a deep gash on her face. She opened her mouth as wide as a depthless pool and gave a blood-chilling cry. Adair covered his ears as the sound threatened to rip his brain in half.

"AGGGGGGHHHHHHHH!!"

He screamed with the witch in pain. His own screams were intermingled with hers. He covered his ears and fell to his knees. Hands colder than a grave gripped his neck.

Two rows of rotten teeth flashed before him burying themselves into his face.

His face ached with pain like it had a heart itself that would burst any moment.

Frantically, he clawed at the hag's face, but her bite held firm, sinking deeper.

He peered into black eyes that were haunted, perhaps by their own reflection or by what they had become. The laughter of the others, clearly still under the witch's spell, rang in his ears.

Selest heard a scream rip the silence. She stumbled out of bed and opened the door, revealing a bloody heap.

"Adair!" she yelled. The wretched creature still held on to his face. He tried to stab her, but her grip remained firm.

Instinctively, Selest grabbed a sharp knife from the table and approached the witch.

Her hands shook uncontrollably. *Asteral, give me strength,* she prayed.

With courage she didn't know she possessed, she grabbed the witch by the hair and slit her throat.

Adair saw her eyes go dim as her bite was released. He shoved the creature away and ran like Hell was at his feet.

His head pounded mercilessly like a hammer upon an anvil. As he regained his composure, he saw Selest trembling, bloody knife in hand.

Almost immediately the spell wore off. Thrion and Faern ceased their laughter and observed the gory scene before them.

The food withered on the platters, and the bright aura that instilled the illusion dimmed.

When they came to their senses, they rushed to Selest and Adair.

"What happened?" Thrion asked. "It seems I've been asleep with my eyes open ever since we sat down to eat."

"S-she poisoned it," explained Selest. "She put you under a spell. We don't know why the Snowess would've done something like that."

Faern peered at the dead figure. It was a hollow corpse with sunken, gaping eyes. "It appears that something took the form of the Winter Virtue. A wielder of Black Magic."

"A witch," Thrion said. "Perhaps she killed Virtue to take on such a form."

"Aye," said Adair with gritted teeth.

Faern helped Adair to his feet. He observed the bite wound marring his face.

Selest rushed to his side. "Adair, are you—?"

"You—" He took her hand, pressed it against his forehead, and bowed. "You saved my life."

She said nothing as she withdrew her hand.

Thrion and Faern peered at her with admiration.

Thrion lowered his head. "She saved mine as well," he sighed, observing the dead witch. "Yet we were foolish." Thrion withdrew his sword, staring at his reflection in its blade.

"We were," Faern said. "We're all prone to make mistakes. We can only learn from our mistakes; only a fool would deny them and try to run away from them."

Thrion sheathed his sword as Faern took stock of the group around him. "Selest has yet to grow into her wings. And Adair is injured. I think we should hold off for about a week, and plan our next course of action. We best fetch our things and make preparations. Who knows if other foul creatures lurk nigh—especially that wretched stag."

Selest trembled at the very thought. "I think I need to—" Sobs wracked her body. "Oh, what have I done?"

Chapter 10

Everyone was startled by her outburst. Thrion quietly approached her. "You saved Adair's life."

"I also *took* a life." She stared at her trembling hands stained with blood.

Adair reeled back, his hand pressed against his facial wound. "That foul witch was in the guise of the Snowess, deceiving many. H-how could you feel—" Faern raised his hand, silencing the dwarf.

The centaur knelt beside her. "I sense there is more at play here, child."

"I-I have never *killed* someone before," she said, squeezing her eyes shut. "I know I did the right thing, but I feel so—different."

Thrion placed his hands on her shoulders steadying her shaking frame.

"'Tis not in your nature. Yet Asteral stirs our hearts beyond our comfort to bring evil to justice. And when justice is done, it brings joy to the righteous and terror to evildoers."

Selest let those words sink in. She sighed. Thrion gave her a gentle hug, mindful of her sprouting wings.

Faern peered in sympathy at the girl. "I know the world you once knew is shattered, and you've lost what you treasured, but take heart, dear one."

Selest relaxed. All three of her new friends made her feel something that she never had felt with her father—closeness. Ever since her mother died, he'd been distant in showing his love for her.

Selest rose. "I think I'm going to rest."

Before returning to her room, she struggled to meet the dwarf's gaze. "I'm truly glad you're all right, Adair. I'm sorry if I offended you in any way."

He waved his hand. "Not to worry. Get some rest, lass."

Once the girl retreated to the comfort of her bed, the others got to work.

Thrion disposed of the foul corpse while Faern salvaged what little supplies they had.

Adair dismissed them and said he would tend to his own wound. "I've dealt with worse," he said.

The three worked the remainder of the evening. They didn't sleep until about midnight or so.

When morning dawned, Thrion rose before the others and went out to the stalls. To his relief, the pony and sleigh were still intact. He searched the stalls and discovered a side door. When he opened it, he was taken aback. Countless saddles and an equine armory lay before him.

The hunter was greeted by a foul stench that made him queasy.

To his horror, behind the stall doors, he found the carcasses of many dead horses. Some even had visible flesh on them, though many were clean to the bone.

He raced back to the house, heart quickening. He burst into the hall and began opening every single door.

All the doors led to bedrooms, but one door revealed a room with skeletons decorated with armor and armed with weapons. The carcasses of dwarves and men littered the floor.

Adair rushed over. "Thrion, what is it that troubles ye?" His eyes widened as he scanned the scene.

"We were not her only victims. 'Tis what I feared."

The dwarf entered the room. He cautiously examined a full fit of armor. "This armor was forged by my people." He observed the unequaled quality of the craftsmanship of his kin. "Not all was lost amidst the Devil's massacre after all. Yet they still met their doom in the clutches of a witch."

In her room, Selest tried to sleep, but the aching feeling on her upper back kept her awake. She flinched at the pain as she tried to get comfortable.

Wearily, she finally rose and observed her forming wings in the full-length mirror.

The dress she wore was of the same raven sheen as her unbound hair. She turned, observing her sprouting arched wings. They were the color of the moon with an ethereal glow.

A knock sounded on the door, startling her.

"Selest, 'tis me, Thrion." Wearily, she approached, opening the door.

Thrion entered, his brow furrowed in concern. "How are you faring? Are your wings still causing pain?"

She nodded. "Just getting used to them is all. What brings you? Is everything all right?"

"Yes. We are gathering provisions for our journey. We are currently gathering weapons and armor. There's an armory here, and I deem it best if you find some of your own for the journey ahead."

"I understand."

Thrion led her to the room they had found.

Within the room, the birch walls were lit by candles setting aglow the silver sheen of armor and mail. To her horror, she observed the skeletons, many of which were men and dwarves; however, she gasped in dismay at the skeletons of the winged folk.

Faern and Adair rummaged through the armory. She stood idly by, watching them fit into chain mail, chest plates, and tested weapons.

Slowly, she walked near a chest plate, lifting it. She caught sight of her reflection in the tarnished metal.

Faern approached. "I don't think that will fit you, Selest. You are much too slim and graceful for armor as bulky as that."

Selest observed a stand adorned in a full set of armor with a long staff as clear as ice.

Her eyes widened. She had read an account of Crysil bearing such a weapon as this—the Longstaff of Ice.

She plucked the breastplate from the stand. Turning it over, she noticed two slits.

The staff rested against the wall nearby. "I guess there's something for me after all." Selest fingered the intricate chains all meticulously linked together. The armor felt surprisingly light.

Thrion approached her. "Try it on. I think it will fit you just fine."

Selest picked up a padded vest. "Explain to me first how I put this on," she said, raising it to her midsection.

"What you have is an arming doublet. The plate of armor goes over it. These arming points are for attaching the plates." He pointed out the laces on the arm sleeves. "You'll then put the studded leather over your arming doublet. There, that's it. Next, put on these leather pants, and then these two poleyns go over your knees."

After Selest followed his instructions, she picked up two dome-shaped plates. "I assume these go on my shoulders?"

Thrion nodded.

"What are they called?"

"Pauldrons." Thrion helped Selest fasten them to her shoulders.

"They feel a bit heavy."

"Ah, you'll get accustomed to your armor in time," Thrion reassured her.

Finally, Selest pulled on a pair of tall leather boots. "What about my wings? Will they grow comfortably into my armor?"

"Don't worry, it won't be a problem. It's why the slits were put in place." She nodded.

She snatched a belt from the stand, fastened it to her waist, and discovered a scabbard that the staff went in. Thrion helped her strap it to her back.

Almost instinctively, she felt her vest pocket. She jerked her head to Thrion. "Do you have the Key?" she whispered.

Thrion retrieved it from his breast pocket, giving it to Selest. She snatched it and stuffed it in her pocket.

She fingered her weapon. It was cold to the touch.

The staff echoed as she tapped it against the marble floor. They stopped what they were doing and observed her with the new weapon.

Adair crossed his arms. "It suits you, Raven."

"Indeed," Thrion said. "It shall serve you well."

"I think with proper training, you will expertly wield the weapon," Faern said.

"You best use this to cover your growing wings, lass," said Adair, handing her a deep blue cloak. "Beyond the Mountain Pass, I fear some will not take kindly to the archangels. You will be exposed to danger. When you are in the Black Icelands, don your cloak, and keep your wings hidden. Your cloak is special. It shall hide your wings, making them invisible to any being who crosses your path."

A chill ran down Selest's spine but she nodded in understanding.

She took the cloak, clasping it about her neck.

"I think I've found something that'll be useful for the next phase of our journey." Faern retrieved a map from a pile of parchment. "I've found a map of the entire Inner Realm," he said, spreading it out on the table.

The centaur observed the map. "We are here," he pointed, "on the edge of Glasefell. I believe the Opal Gate isn't too far away."

Selest's heart skipped a beat. In a poem titled "Garnet Teardrops" it was said during the Thaw, an Opal Gate was set in between lands of winter and spring. It was meant to delineate the border of Snow and Mist, where the Glacian King fell. The gate's embedded garnets represented the blood of those who died resisting the Ice King.

"If we start early in the morning," Thrion continued, "we should reach the Enchanted Forest tomorrow late in the evening."

Faern turned to Adair. "What dangers will we face?"

"Only the demons near the mountains," he said. "I wouldn't be surprised if the fall of my kin has emboldened them. It would be wise if we stayed as far away from the mountains as possible. We should be wary regardless of my familiarity with this territory." He shivered. "We have yet to discover what other horrors lurk."

"We should also be wary of Icen Boars as well. They dwell in the Black Icelands, not too far away from here," said Thrion.

"How far are we from the Opal Gate?" asked Selest.

Thrion looked at the map. "On horseback, we should be able to cover forty miles in a day, if not more. And from here to the Opal Gate, it should be about a six-day journey; five at the least."

Selest observed the company suited in their new armor. Thrion bore the same cloak as before, and Adair's worn blue cloak draped off his shoulders. The centaur carried his curved saber, and Thrion, his sword. Adair had a long dagger found amidst the dwarven weapons, along with Emei daggers fastened upon his belt. He also bore rings of tiny blades.

They exited the armory and rested in their rooms for a final night.

The next morning they prepared to leave. Counting their provisions for the journey, they discovered they had enough to last three days.

"There'll be game we can hunt to last us the few remaining days," reassured Thrion.

After rationing out the food amongst themselves, they mounted the sleigh and began to depart.

The black pony trotted merrily along, delighted to be on the road again.

And with one final look behind them, they started for the path into the forest, riding in single file; Adair driving the sleigh, and Faern taking the rear.

Selest dared a glimpse back to Crysil's home marveling at how far they had come. Thrion had said they should reach the Golden Fields of Orai in less than a week.

She fingered the Key, recalling her father's words. Her mother's dying wish was to see the door of Fhar locked. Sighing, she looked ahead. Whatever was to come, she prayed their suffering would not be in vain.

Chapter 11

One early morning, Adair guided them up a steep slope. Thrion sat beside the dwarf, discussing their route. Selest focused on the horses' hooves crunching the snow as they trotted upward.

A rhythmic beat was in her ears.

One-two...One-two...One-two...

It sounded in sync with her heart as she tried to take her mind off the new burden upon her back.

Four days had passed. During that time, Selest felt her wings grow and form into their full length.

Not wanting to disturb the other two, she turned to the centaur.

"Faern?" she asked.

"Yes?"

"Is it true that people don't take kindly to archangels because of the past?"

A heavy silence filled the air.

Finally, he spoke. "I don't mean to worry you, but it's best to be cautious in times like these."

Selest's heart quickened.

"From the western oaks of the Enchanted Forest to the foul kingdom of Shadenfell, many perceive winged folk as bad omens sent by Asteral to bring judgment upon them."

"So they want nothing to do with their Creator?"

"Yes. They blame Him for their downfall. But really it was their own doing. So for the time being just keep your wings hidden beneath your cloak, and when we leave this forest you'll be safe in the Golden Fields."

She sighed. "I fear it has become more difficult." Her wings were likely ten feet in length now, she guessed. "That is why I am glad I have something to defend myself with," she said, glancing at her staff.

"You shall put it to good use soon enough," Faern said.

As they rode, she observed ice beads forming white blankets of snow guarded by great towering pines.

"What do you think lies ahead, Faern?"

To her surprise, the centaur chuckled. "You think far into the future, little Owl Wing."

Her face grew red. "I suppose it's because I'm afraid."

"Ah!" Faern gave her a reassuring look. "We must focus on the present. If we don't, then we lose sight of missed opportunities. Though that's not to say I don't have my fair share of worrying; I choose to hold true to the present. I fear for the future just as much. But fear is only a part of being. Without fear, bravery would be absent."

"I—never have taken that into account."

"Asteral wants us to look for the better in the face of the worst. After all, He is for us, is He not?"

Selest smiled.

The path began to curve and slope downward. Selest remained silent, contemplating his words.

The sun dawned high and pale as the company continued. Not a sign of life was present—for the time being at least. When luncheon came about, they each helped themselves to whatever was in their possession: frozen berries, pine nuts, and seeds. And to their surprise, it satisfied their hunger.

After traversing many more miles they made camp in the shelter of the fir trees early in the evening.

While Thrion hunted for game and Adair collected herbs, Faern trained with Selest.

"Tell me Selest, do you—or have you—done much stargazing?" Faern asked, curiosity blooming on his face as they took a break from their exercises.

Selest looked to the sky cut out of the outline of the pine tops. She could just barely make out the stars in the evening sky.

"'Twas during Starry Eve when we celebrated the stars." An ache pounded against her rib cage—longing for what had passed, perhaps, when all was fair and enchanting.

"Ah, the celebration of the faerie lights." Faern focused his attentive gaze on the unseen stars as well.

Selest started. "You celebrated the occasion likewise?"

"Of course." He settled his eyes on her. "But to my people, it's known by a different name: Fae's Eve."

Questions dawned in Selest's thoughts like a new blue moon. "What is your history of the fae and the centaurs?"

The centaur grew thoughtful. "They are our guardians sent from the heavens." His gaze fixed once more upon the sky. "At times, they appear as stars high in the sky, yet also seem in reach. On rare occasions they can be found upon the forest floor, wreathed in the mist; just faint glowing lights pulsing like a heartbeat." Now everyone was drawn to the entrancing tale.

Faern continued. "They have only appeared in the realm when tidings were most dire. Sometimes as the whispering of air beneath leaves, other times the crystal chime of rippling waters, but also an enchanting song ever so faint."

"Have you ever seen one?" asked Selest.

Faern bowed his head. "Nay." He paused for a long, it seemed grieving, moment. "But my dam had."

He cleared his throat before telling the company the treacherous account.

"Long ago," he began, "my dam told me the tale that gave me my name. When she was carrying me, she was frolicking in the Emerald Dells, overjoyed by my coming, knowing at the time she was carrying a son. Blinded by her happiness, she wandered too far and reached the borderlands of the Shile. The Eleven pursued her."

He paused while a lump formed in his throat. "She fled for her life, but the Eleven ran her down. She fought death as she was meeting it, and as it was about to take her like a passing breath, a faerie appeared to her in her darkest hour. She described the fae as a being with iridescent wings, crystal clear to the eye, yet small in size, cast in a rainbow glow. The ethereal guardian warded off the evil present and healed my dam's wounds. Then it aided her in labor. When she gave birth, she named me Faern as a reminder of the fae's aid. And from that day hence I remember when my dam and I peered at the stars on the horizon of the Emerald Dells. I remember the conversation we shared. When I glanced at my dam staring intently at the stars I asked her, 'Why do you gaze at that star as if it were a god?'

"She simply smiled at me and said, 'Because it saved my life, and I am grateful for it, but I do not worship it.'

"I asked her, 'Yes, but do you know who put it there?'

"She replied, 'Our Creator, Asteral: the one who sent the fae to save me. We should give thanks to the Creator, not the created.'

"It has been a reminder to me ever since." He choked on his words like choking on a bitter memory. "She would always tell me, 'No matter what happens, look to the Fae Star, Faern, and do not let your gaze falter. For it is the same star that Asteral created to be a beacon for us all in our darkest hours. Never forget.'"

He peered at the timeless stars. "And I never have."

Selest pondered his words as she peered at the starry sky above.

She was relieved to know she was not alone in her grief.

For a second, a vision of her father's face flashed before her eyes; the same deep thunder-colored hair and his cold blue eyes glazed in pure terror.

She noticed Adair peering south to the mountain range, knowing he was looking at his old home. Her heart stirred for the dwarf.

Thrion shifted uneasily. She saw deep anger kindling within his eyes. It was a silent flame ever-growing, fueled by the others' grief. He wrapped his fingers tightly on the hilt of his sword, muscles tense. Selest's eye caught the swift movement.

"T-Thrion?" Selest put a calming hand on his. He relaxed. "Does Faern's story stir your heart so?"

"Did ye spy something peculiar?" Adair eyed the hunter. "Or are ye just fighting some internal conflict?"

Thrion exhaled a mournful sigh. "You have discerned correctly. Deep within, the centaur's tale had a great effect on my heart."

"Well, for that I am grateful," said Faern.

"Aye, it opened my eyes for the better," agreed the dwarf.

"Indeed it did." Selest lowered her head. "Thrion, I have also pondered your wisdom. Worrying about the future is one thing, but worrying about the past is endless. You don't have to worry about uncertainty because everything in the past has already taken place. What frightens me is repeating the same mistakes of the past, and thus ruining the future."

"All in His time, lass, all in His time," Adair said.

Weariness overcame them as the evening continued to fade to twilight, casting the pines into shadow.

The quarter moon's face winked like a pale dish.

Already Thrion had the kindling ablaze. The others circled around crackling flames.

Selest settled beside Adair, huddling in her cloak as she let the fire warm her frozen flesh.

Her three companions stared intently at the flames.

Selest unsheathed her staff, examining it in the moonlight. The staff of ice glimmered like a frozen raindrop.

Despite the heat that emanated from the fire, the staff remained cold to the touch.

She turned the long, slender weapon over in her hands. She watched the light dance and glitter in the firelight. It seemed to reflect the stars and moon overhead, crisp and clear.

She caught a mirror image of herself within the icy staff: her blue hair with its raven sheen, and her dark eyes glittering in starlight against pale skin.

"Are we still on for more training, Faern? Or is it too late in the night?"

"Tonight, I say instead of working on technique, I think you are ready for a sparring lesson."

Selest jolted, breaking out of her reverie. "With you?"

"Adair shall be your first opponent. What you lack in strength you make up for with speed and agility. As of now, you're not strong enough to spar with me."

The dwarf scrambled to his feet, unsheathing his long dagger.

Selest noticed Thrion sitting, arms crossed. He nodded toward her, eyes twinkling.

Her hands trembled. "I—I don't know if I'm ready for this."

Adair chuckled. "Ye think I was good enough to win my first sparring session, Raven?"

Selest smiled. "N-no. I suppose not."

"It's all right, lass. No harm will come to ya," Adair reassured her.

Selest removed her cloak exposing her wings. She gripped her weapon in both hands and assumed a fighting stance.

Faern had told her to think of the staff as an extension of her arm. She placed her left hand up, and right hand down, making sure her grip was weighted in the middle, hand length apart.

Selest inhaled, the air stinging her lungs. Exhaling, she placed all her focus on her opponent. The dwarf was clad in his mail. She needed an opening.

Adair remained patient; watching, waiting like a wolf hunting its prey.

Selest hesitated.

Adair lunged forward, dagger raised. She dodged out of the way, swinging for his head. Adair blocked the blow, seizing the end of her staff.

The dwarf jerked the weapon from her hands.

"You cannot hesitate," said Faern. "Already it cost you your weapon. Your tactics are predictable. You must be more creative than that."

Adair pointed the staff at her. Selest inched away.

Without warning, Adair lunged.

Dodging the blow, she scooped up a ball of snow and threw it at his face. Adair stopped, wiping the snow off his beard.

She took her chance. Grabbing her staff, she quickly regained her composure.

"You seize the opportunity, at best," the dwarf mused. He dashed for her.

Selest extended her staff, swinging for his legs.

Adair jumped, the staff narrowly missing its mark.

The knife clanged against the staff. Adair leaned forward pressing against her. Selest gritted her teeth, trying to stand her ground. But the dwarf's strength could not be matched.

In a flash, Selest leaped back. The dwarf fell face-first into the snow.

Selest stumbled backward, panting for breath.

The dwarf regained his composure, charging toward her. Selest gasped. As she flexed her wings, the wind picked up. Selest's breath caught in her throat as she jumped back, wings extended in response.

An arctic breeze rose in her wake and caught beneath her wings.

Her heart jumped off a great height. Selest was airborne, rising above her companions' heads!

She spread her arms wide, her staff sliding from her fingers. The feeling of weightlessness took her breath away. As she peered up at the stars, she had a momentary escape from the world below.

"Selest, retract your wings!" Faern cried, trotting after her. The centaur's thundering voice startled her. She jerked her head down in panic toward the snowy landscape masked in pines.

"Easy, easy," he coaxed her down.

She retracted her wings all too suddenly in the midst of her panic and began falling.

Her head jerked upward once more. She faced the sky as she spread her wings, lifting onto an unseen swell, resurfacing to meet a greater ocean. Floating higher into the air, now well above the treetops, but this time gradually retracting her wings, she descended.

The centaur reared and took Selest's hands, helping her down.

She landed softly, and shakily released a breath she didn't know she was holding.

"D-did I—?"

"By Celtan's Bow, you have scared me half to death," Faern laughed.

"I—" She stared at the ground as if she was afraid of the sheer white blankness as it seemed to engulf her.

He handed Selest her staff. "Did your wings hurt when you found yourself airborne?"

"No. I only felt like I could stay in the air for a while."

"Breathe now, child," Faern said. "Just breathe."

"It seems we have accomplished more than what we bargained for." Adair peered up at her with a new look of approval. "Not bad for yer first fight. I also see the exercises I've given ya are paying off."

Selest opened and closed her wings. "The exercises you've suggested are strengthening them."

Adair's eyes twinkled with admiration. "The more you exercise them, the stronger they'll be."

Faern and Adair laughed. She peered at Thrion. His expression was in a state of shock. "We've had quite an eventful evening. Best we should get some rest while the night is young."

Faern nodded and trotted to the fireside, kneeling with great weariness. "We have a long road ahead of us yet."

Selest felt a heaviness upon her brow settling like a circlet of gold.

She turned toward heavy footsteps crunching in the snow behind her.

Adair kept pace with her long strides.

"Well, Raven, ye did well tonight."

She gave him a sidelong glance. "You think so?"

With a nod, Adair retreated to his place beside the fire. "We'll make a fine warrior outta ya. Just wait and see."

He lay outstretched on his boar-skin cloak, drinking in the stars. "'Yer just a young lad, Aide, in an old world, under a timeless sky.' 'Twas what me Da always told me."

Selest settled beside him, following the dwarf's gaze.

Adair continued to peer at the stars for some time, then fell asleep.

"Under a timeless sky," Selest whispered the words like an icicle dripping in the fresh breezes of spring. She lay down as stars drifted in her mind's eye.

She saw Thrion tend to the fire, as the sparks cracked and popped in reply. "Seems their little training session tuckered them out," he whispered to Faern.

"You best get some rest," Faern said. "I'll take the first watch."

Nodding, Thrion settled into a sleeping position. "Very well. Good night, Faern."

The moon hung high in the sky, shining in a still night. The wind ceased to blow. The only sound Faern heard was the snoring of the dwarf and the snorting of the black pony.

Sighing, the centaur peered at the moon and thought of his home. Perhaps the same moon shone there. He observed the constellation of Celtan's starry bow, aimed at a void target, leaving gaping holes of light in its wake like a shooting star.

For the first time in years, ever since the centaur's dam was slain, silent tears rolled down Faern's cheeks.

Chapter 12

Black faded to deep violet. The morning's first glow awoke the travelers from distant dreams. They observed the purple morn, the moon behind the mountains' rocky curtain.

The sky was veiled in splashes of deep wine and violet which cast a magenta aura through Twilforest. The sight transfixed them.

Selest noticed Faern rousing near the dying embers.

She saw Thrion sitting on a nearby rock, bow in hand, deep in thought. His fingers traced his short-trimmed beard and he looked like a philosopher enjoying the morning's solitude.

"Any suspicious activity?" yawned Adair.

"Nay. All is as quiet as an abandoned house."

When everyone awoke, they ate a quick breakfast of berries and a rabbit that Thrion had shot and then continued their journey.

Adair led them up a steep ridge masked in pine trees.

Their eyes slowly took in the Opal Gate against the dark gray sky. The gate loomed high before them, engraved in the mountains.

As they approached, the gate came closer into view. Its doors were lined with black spades, pointing upwards. Etched in the posts were red garnets.

Selest stared at the gate in awe.

Thrion tried the ringed latch. "It's locked," he said. They peered above. "There's no way we could climb."

"If only there was a way to unlock the door," Selest said.

"Of course," said Thrion, looking at her. "Selest, the Key. Try sliding it into the door."

Selest retrieved the Key and did just that. She twisted it and heard a *click!* as she turned the latch and opened the door.

Adair urged the pony forward, maneuvering the sleigh past the gate and onto dry ground. "The sleigh will be of no more use for us here," he said. "'Tis best to leave it and travel with the pony." They placed their belongings onto the pony before Adair led it forward as they continued on their way.

Before her, Selest noticed that the land was dotted with trees—tall oaks covered in moss instead of the pines and evergreens they left behind. She saw a yuletide mint with an aura of silver. Yet not a living thing stirred.

Later that evening they ate a quiet supper of rabbit meat and wild berries.

"How are yer wounds?" asked Adair, between a munch of berries. He peered at the gash in Faern's hide.

"Better," replied Faern. "That Evenmint sure does the trick."

"What about you, lass, yer wounds any better?"

"Same as Faern." She quietly added, "Though I'll never forget the biting cold of Emberthel."

Adair nodded understandingly, feeling his bite wound. "And yer wings?"

"It's a matter of getting accustomed to them." Selest grasped at the scapula of her left wing. "They feel heavy—almost like a…"

Adair raised an eyebrow.

She lowered her head. "Burden."

"They are a marking of your people, child," Faern said firmly. "You have the gift of flight and are best to think of it that way." She stared at the centaur.

"You don't understand—"

"Your wings are not a burden," Thrion snapped. "Faern is right, they are a gift." He peered longingly at the sky. "To fly, to be able to rise up and marvel at the stars, that is a gift to treasure." A hint of grief was evident in his voice.

Selest glanced up at the gray sky in a painful reality. How could she have been so blind? Were they truly a gift?

"Well, the wasteland is behind us now, I think we should get some rest," Faern said.

Later that night, Adair tended to the pony, while Faern and Thrion studied the map. Selest took the first watch.

After they settled down for the night, all was quiet, except for the occasional soft whinny of the pony.

Thrion took the second watch.

Selest tossed and turned, finally getting up and joining Thrion by the fire.

"Thrion?" she whispered.

"Hmm?" he said, startled out of his fancy. "Spot anything out of the ordinary?"

"It's not that I am concerned about."

"Well then, what is it?"

She looked around the pale-lit mossy oaks draped in a gray hue, similar to The Glade's, but with more mist, and the color a refreshing Yuletide green. She inhaled the vapors. "This place reminds me of The Glade. The trees make me recall my own front yard where all of our neighbors would come and celebrate Starry Eve."

Thrion looked around at the untrodden land. "'Twas the time my father came bearing ill news, was it not?"

Selest recalled the distant memory.

Adair interjected, "The Glade—ye mean to say yer from Sovoria, lass?"

"I—yes. I'm from that region." She shook her head. "I—I haven't heard that name in so long. My father never mentioned the name. He only referred to The Glade."

Thrion stroked his beard, deep in thought. "Your father was a secretive man. He likely ne'er brought up Sovoria because he wanted to keep your origin as an archangel secret."

She sighed. "I know. I just wish he would've told me so it didn't all come as such a shock."

Thrion placed his hands on her shoulders, looking her square in the eye. "Your father's intent was to protect you by keeping it a secret."

A sting of betrayal cut through her like a knife. "I—wish he hadn't."

Thrion pulled her into an embrace. "What's done is done, lass—all you can do now is look ahead."

She nodded, withdrawing from the hug. "I think I just need to rest." She smiled. "Goodnight."

Thrion nodded. "Goodnight."

The moon gleamed as a waxing gibbous. The gray blanket of the early morn brought forth mists, dampening the earth.

Selest shivered as she awoke. A bright glint caught her eye. An unearthly echo followed.

Tra-la-lay
Alone, astray
Fa-la-lay
Dawn, day
La-le-lay
Follow, Fae

The singing faerie startled and turned to face her. She met the faerie's ghostly gaze of a pale blue light with an unaged face, for all the age within it was in its dark eyes. The faerie stared not at her but *through* her.

Immediately she recalled the centaur's story of a fae that saved his mother from death while being hunted by the Eleven.

A flash of sapphire zipped past her.

A trail of faes formed before her.

Selest was tempted to follow. She rushed toward Thrion. She startled him from his thoughts.

"Thrion."

"What is it? See anything peculiar?"

"Yes, I spotted quite an odd sight."

"What?"

"Faerie," she whispered. "We must tell the others."

"Selest—how can you be so certain?" Before Thrion could say anything more she rushed to Faern.

"Faern." The centaur started from a deep sleep.

"What is it?" He looked about, fingering his hilt, expecting the enemy to strike.

"I saw a fae."

"What's wrong?" Adair roused from his slumber.

"Really?" asked Faern at the same time. For the first time, Selest saw excitement kindle in his eyes.

"I saw a fae wreathed in mist," she replied.

She turned and pointed to where he stood. "The faerie was blue in color, and I was certain I could make out a fair face. It seemed to pay me no mind, and then simply vanished into the oaks." She pointed to the far left of the trees.

"The faerie, a herder of spirits," said Faern, deep in thought.

"I read in a book back home that they make themselves unseen to others unless they wish to be seen," mused Selest.

"It could be a trap no doubt," said the dwarf.

Silence covered the group as each was lost in thought.

Finally, Faern asked, "What did the fae seem to say?"

Selest creased her brow in thought. "I can't rightly recall at the moment. It was all a whisper really." She paused. "All I remember is it being a sort of rhyme. All I could get out of it was *dawn, day,* and *follow fae.*" Everyone gave a start.

"Where did it disappear to?"

"In that group of trees yonder," she said, nodding in the direction of the gate. Now the trees shimmered as if in a mirage of mist. It had an eerie feel to it—at least, a feeling they were unaccustomed to. It wasn't a temptation, but a sort of salutation.

"This place better not be as terrible as what lay behind the gate."

They glanced over the landscape. The sight sent shivers down their spines. An eerie quietness was upon the lands, a grayness as if torn between good and evil.

"It's like we are in a land rid of evil things, though it has an odd air to it, and we are just not acquainted with the forest," observed Selest. "I do not know if you all feel this way, but I most certainly do."

Adair nodded looking about. "In a way, yes."

"Maybe it's the opposite of how we felt in the witch's realm; a deceiving sort of safeness, and perhaps—though we feel insecure in this place—maybe we are just deceiving ourselves," she continued.

"Maybe you have a point there, child."

After a short while, they heard the faintest snap of a twig. They sat stone still. Selest gripped her staff.

Another snapped…

And another…

Whatever it was, was drawing closer.

Selest strained to see into the shadowed trees, and could just make out a faint bent-over shape. Her eyes widened; her shoulders tensed.

Suddenly, the wind picked up amidst the stillness. The breeze sent shivers down their spines.

"I knew something was amiss," said Selest. "I don't know about you all, but I feel the source coming from those trees."

Faern unsheathed his sword. "I won't take any chances." Patiently they waited—until a shadow appeared.

They drew their weapons, poised to strike.

Closer and closer it came. From afar, they made out a black-cloaked figure with a pale face folded in many wrinkles, the etching of many years. An orange light seemed to float beside it. Not until their eyes caught a glint of silver did they realize it bore a lantern. And so it was that they beheld an old woman.

Chapter 13

In the pale morn, orange light cast a hollow aura around the woman's ancient frame which emanated silent intimidation.

Selest froze as she felt the aquamarine eyes rest upon her. The old lady had iridescent blue butterfly-like wings.

Her hair was white as snow and framed her pale face. Her garments were white, with stag furs draped over her stooped figure.

She bore an arched staff where a citrine lantern hung.

After a moment of silence, she opened her cracked lips and spoke in a thin voice.

"Who are you?"

Faern straightened to his full height. "We're refugees from the West."

The ancient woman peered at the gate as if recalling a distant memory. "Many have been cast under her spell, and eaten by the vile witch," she murmured.

Selest shivered. "W-who are *you*?" she asked. The old woman turned to her.

Selest tensed under her keen gaze. She felt exposed, as though this woman knew her better than she knew herself.

"I am Etris, Faekeeper, and Crysil's former apprentice." She peered at the gate. "Long has it been since any have crossed that gateway. Though I must admit, this is quite a strange party indeed; a centaur, dwarf, man, and a girl."

She paused. "The faeries told me of something peculiar hereabouts. How did you escape her spell?"

"Well, not all were under the witch's spell." Faern stepped back, gazing admirably at Adair and Selest.

"What is your name, child?" the woman asked.

Selest stared at Faern, hesitating. He nodded. Selest stepped forth more boldly than she felt inside. "My name is Selestial, daughter of Savion Inriser."

Blue eyes looked at her with admiration. "You wear Crysil's armor and bear her Longstaff of Ice."

Selest's face grew red. "My apologies, my lady, I didn't mean—"

Etris smiled. "Well-deserved for a young warrior such as yourself. Now comes the rest of you, to whom do I owe the pleasure?"

Faern bowed. "Faern Dawnback, son of Faeodin, at your service."

Adair flexed his hand, staring down at the foliage. "Adair Echodeep, at yours."

Selest noticed Thrion hanging back.

The old woman squinted past her.

"Who is he who lingers in the shadows?"

She strode toward him. To Selest's surprise, he turned away. "Forgive me, my lady, but I fear I am unworthy to be in your presence."

Startled, the old woman peered deep into his eyes.

"I know your eyes, yet they are etched with the age of manhood. Thrion Silveran, you remind me so much of your father."

Thrion turned away. "I'm nothing like my father."

"Why do you continue to decay inward, due to this self-made revelation?"

Thrion bowed his head. "I failed. My father will be waiting at Orai with refugees from the West. I was to bring as many as I could. He placed his trust in me."

He stole a glance at Selest. "The one I was entrusted to protect nearly lost her life because of me."

Selest approached him. "I was willing to sacrifice my life for you, Thrion. It wasn't your fault," Selest told him firmly. "And you can't blame yourself for the actions of my people. They chose to remain oblivious to the coming of the witches—"

"And they're dead because of it!" he yelled. "The West is lost."

Selest withdrew the Key from her pocket. Faern and Adair started forward. She paid no heed. She held it up to him, forcing him to look at it. "We hold the Key to fulfill Asteral's promise. So please, don't lose hope."

At that moment, the wind picked up, slicing through Selest's skin.

She looked up and saw the dark base of looming storm clouds.

"Pack up your camp, and let us take our leave. A storm brews on the horizon," said Etris. "I shall provide you shelter for the remainder of the day." She raised her lantern, enveloping them in a warm light.

Thrion walked past Selest. "My faith has dwindled. That token means nothing." He covered her hand holding the Key and squeezed. "I'm happy if it brings you any, though."

He turned to the others, letting go of her hand. "Come, let's break camp."

Selest placed the Key back in her pocket with a sigh.

Faern approached her, placing a hand on her shoulder. "Give him time. Pray his heart will be given to Asteral in his dire hour."

Selest forced a smile. "I will."

The others retreated back to their campsite. "How can we trust you?" asked Adair, saddling his pony.

"I have not yet killed you have I?" Etris peered into his eyes. "A friend of

Yaelas' son is a friend of mine. Besides, the faes of this forest can lead one off the path, making one lost, and I am the only one who knows this forest."

Adair raised an eyebrow, looking expectantly at the centaur. "Well, whaddya say to that?"

"I deem it best to follow Etris. And I trust Yaelas' judgment," said Faern. "And if she is a friend to Yaelas, then I trust her."

Selest shivered. "And I wouldn't mind having some proper shelter for once."

Adair hesitated. "Ye swear ye won't betray me or any of my friends?"

The faekeeper nodded. "Lest your intentions pertain to greed and bloodshed."

Adair opened his mouth, but snapped his jaw shut, considering. Then, he held up his right hand. "Do you swear, unless we prove ill to your home?"

Etris raised her right hand in turn. "I swear by the mighty Asteral's hand."

Adair nodded in agreement. They turned to follow the faekeeper deeper into the forest.

Etris walked slowly, as though she had all the time in the world.

Faern traveled beside Etris. Thrion and Selest walked side by side, while Adair led the pony, taking up the rear.

The company left the Opal Gate behind. It stood desolate, its embedded garnets twinkling in the faerie light.

Selest observed the forest about her. The trees certainly did have an enchanted feel to them, yet not at all evil and deceiving like Twil. Though a wonderland, it had ended up being a frozen wasteland after all. Instead of a Yule mint, this forest had a floral fae-green sort of color. And it indeed made all feel enchanted, yet not at all surreal, but—tangible.

The travelers unexpectedly found themselves in shock, like waking up from a dream into reality. The surreality of the West left them as they suddenly became aware of their surroundings as if for the first time. The sights, sounds, and smells came into sharper focus than the pilgrims had ever experienced before. Scoping out the trees, they made out the faintest of pale lights.

"Do not heed the fae lights or else you shall stray off the path."

"Is that their intent?" asked Selest.

Etris raised her lantern. "They are drawn to the light, as it acts like the sun. Wherever I go, they follow. It is their nature."

"It mustn't be all that lonely as a faekeeper then," said Selest.

"No, it is not. They are my dearest friends, for they were under Crysil's authority."

Selest pondered this. "So the faeries of Crysil live on?"

The keeper went silent.

The fae lights dimmed. Finally, she drew a long, sad breath. "Faeries are part of a Virtue. And that fragment gets carried on with the apprentice. Yet, the memory forever haunts us. Long ago, when Crysil was murdered by the very Temptress who imitated her heavenly form, the light of the gray faes haunted the forest in mourning."

Faern observed the faes. "So it was the Temptress who exiled you from your mistress' fair realm?"

Etris sighed. "Indeed, Master Centaur—the faes and I alike." She looked at the sky, not a gray storm, but a clear, blue sky. "Ah yes, they once danced like snowflakes and flurries in the pale winter sun. Oh, how they would dazzle in the light. Such elegant and graceful beings they were."

Her joy faded. "They were a part of her, the faes. Once she died, they faded from the sky and snow, and fell upon the forest floor, ne'er to grace the skies again."

They continued on in silence for some time, following the orange light of the faekeeper. The trees and the wisps' lights about them remained constant. Selest peered in amusement at the forest as it had a magical, playful feel to it.

They halted before a small opening in the trees. In the center of the clearing, Selest beheld a granite birdbath.

"Why have we stopped?" asked Faern.

"I tend to the Mirror of High Seer," she said. "This is my daily routine."

"What might one see?" Curiosity bloomed deep within Selest.

"One can see a thousand specters, true and yet untrue: past, present, future through and through. The past is certain, the present constant, but the future," she peered into their eyes, "is another matter. The future is only what we make it. Foreseers only predict, as do prophecies. We are the swayers of a future, uncertain. Gather round, if you care to witness my work."

They all sat before the bath, Etris standing above it, peering in. The lights gathered around the ring of the trees as well. Some of the more adventurous ones inched closer to the travelers.

The refugees startled at the creeping lights, scrambling closer together. Adair itched to draw his weapon.

"Stay your blade, they are only curious as to why you are here." Quietly Etris added, "Remember the oath you swore, Master Dwarf."

The keeper raised her lantern above the face of the bath and placed it in the pool's center.

The water appeared crystal clear, mirroring the sky and the treetops from above. One could only be certain that they could drown within the stillness, and stand within the small realm.

She raised the lantern from the water. "We shall remain in the present, for the mirror only predicts what could be."

She peered at them in a warning. "Whate'er is shown, don't touch the water, or else you'll lose yourself in its depths."

All grew unearthly quiet. Even the fae lights dimmed. She stared at each with penetrative eyes.

"Many years I have watched the stars," said Etris, "and have pondered upon them as many times."

"As have I," replied Faern. "As they are yours to watch, I have peered upon His remnant."

"Many have, my young stargazer," Etris replied. "The triadic star foretells His coming, as it says in your fantasy."

Selest startled. "Keeper, why the lack of faith?"

Etris peered west, as if beyond the Opal Gate. "My faith is in the life of the trees and the soul of pure light. My faith is buried with her."

Raising her lantern, she opened a small glass door, retrieving orange light as pixie dust, it seemed, and sprinkled it upon the water's surface. She swirled it around along with the water without even touching the surface. The gray sky with shadows of the treetops overhead spiraled out of distorted whorls and merged into ink, floating with orange stars scattered throughout the expanse.

The image shifted. They looked down upon a massive silver door. Behind were mountains that mirrored the door's ethereal hue. Above it, the stars of their world appeared as a dome. The surface was only glass, but from the light reflected off of it glowed a two-pointed star. Many colors of different hues danced upon the surface and shimmered in the sky as an aurora until the colors came together into the form of a key.

The color in Selest's face drained.

They all beheld the sight in awestruck wonder.

The image grew dark as the door decayed from silver to gray until it was a still pool of water once more.

Eerily, a distant wail howled from the trees. They jerked their heads in that direction, trying to discern who or what caused it.

"By my beard," breathed Adair. "Ne'er have I dreamed of the day when I'd look upon the Silver Mountains of Dwindleoth. But the Door which was forged by my ancestors—that is another thing entirely."

Etris peered at the company in alarm. "Ne'er have I seen such a vision."

"What does it mean?" asked Thrion.

"It means the time is nigh. The Prophecy of Asteral is to be fulfilled in this Era."

Selest grasped the Key in her pocket.

"Heed my words, travelers, and keep them in your mind, and not your heart, for the heart is tangled with emotion and pride." She turned. "Come. Time is fraying by a thread."

"Where will you lead us?" Adair questioned, his brow creased.

She halted and glanced at the dwarf. "To Crysil's grave, son of Darragh." They followed behind her, leaving the birdbath shrouded in the mist.

Chapter 14

Many silent miles had been trodden when the trees began to thin. An old church came into view. It was cloaked in gray mist, creating a mournful forgetting.

"'Twas a chapel once," said Etris, "where many a passerby and I would gather for fellowship. Now, it is a forgotten tomb."

Selest shivered at her words. "So Crysil is buried there?"

"Entombed, yes." Etris nodded. "After the Temptress, the most vile of her kind, killed my mentor, I deemed it best to entomb her in what was once my chapel. Now, I tend to her grave."

Fear crawled up Selest's spine as she realized this is where Etris intended for them to stay for the night.

As they got closer, Selest discerned gray statues frozen with outstretched wings.

A look of silent wisdom was etched in each of their frozen expressions. She touched the cold cheek of an archangel and peered into its eyes in the bleak mist. She traced her fingers down the back, and across the engraved feathers of the great wings. Faern and Adair stood staring in speculation. Thrion peered in wonder as he beheld their timeless faces.

A deep sorrow tugged at Selest's heart as she felt the archangels' pain emanating from within the stone exterior.

"Ne'er have I beheld such a mournful solitude," mused Faern.

"Most winged folk of Twil were banned or killed by the Temptress," replied Etris.

They continued through the plain studded with statues until they reached the building.

"Selest, come on!" yelled Faern, as they retreated into the dwelling. She noticed the pony had been tethered underneath a small awning.

She followed, guided by the entrancing citrus glow of the keeper's lantern. She peered behind her as the first rain poured down.

When Selest entered the chapel, now a sepulcher, she noticed in the center lay a stone coffin encrusted with garnets. Wine-colored rose petals were scattered about the tomb, creating a musky fragrance. The atmosphere was heavy with mourning. Stone walls grew dark in the waning sunlight. A single narrow window created a shaft of light that shone upon the gray stone of the tomb she assumed to be Crysil's.

The rain pattered on the roof like a troop of mice skittering overhead.

Etris raised her lantern so that it cast orange shadows about the tomb. Selest squinted at the message engraved upon the stone.

In winter lands, a rose shall wither
Ere break of the day come hither
All is was and will be forsaken
In the golden light awaken
The dark that dwells will be forbidden
In His remnant shall be unhidden

"It is a fragment of a hymn long forgotten. It was Crysil's favorite."

Selest caught a tinge of sadness in her voice. "What does the hymn speak of?" she asked.

The keeper peered at the lovely face engraved in the stone. "Of a coming hope."

"What is the coming hope, do you suppose?" asked Selest.

"The hope is those who choose to stand against evil," replied the keeper. "There our hope must reside."

She gazed out the narrow window to the blinding gray. "Long ago, false prophets infiltrated this sacred place, spinning a myth called fate."

She turned to look intently at Selest. "When you take your leave tomorrow, be wary; false prophets will emerge to sweep you away. Do not heed their words. Instead, study them, and observe their actions. Only then will their true colors surface." She sat on a stone slab. "From here, until you reach the Golden Fields, temptations will sway you."

"We'll heed your words," replied Faern.

"I am glad to hear. Now meditate on these words as you take your rest. And by dawn's first light, you must be on your way."

Everyone settled for the remainder of the evening, enjoying a quiet supper of the remains of rabbit meat from the previous night's dinner.

Etris offered some berries and mushrooms native to the forest. She also offered them rainwater she had collected from outside.

After they ate, they broke into small groups. Adair supervised Selest's wing exercises, while Etris and Faern discussed the next step of their journey. Thrion remained in a far corner, peering intently out the narrow window.

Selest's heart hurt for him. *Asteral, please open his heart, let him see that it wasn't his fault.* "You can't blame yourself for others' actions," she whispered.

"Hm?" Adair furrowed his brow. "Ye said somethin' lass?"

She sighed, gesturing for Thrion. "I'm worried about him. I hate seeing him so—sad."

"Give him time. He'll come around."

A tear escaped her eye. "I hope you're right."

She unclasped her cape and draped it over the stone slab, lying down on the chilling surface. The rain kept falling.

Adair rose. "I best have all my medical supplies accounted for before we leave on the morrow. Let me know if ye need anything." The dwarf left Selest deep in thought. She stared intently at Thrion, praying, hoping his saddened gaze would cease.

She sniffed, wiping away the tears. Perhaps, she thought, it'd be best if she got some sleep. In spite of her cloak, the cold from the stone seeped through her skin. She shivered, spreading her wings to create a cocoon of warmth.

She noticed Thrion's eyes resting on her. He wasn't looking at her but through her, as though he was reminiscing about something he had lost. He turned back to the window.

The voices of Faern and Etris rang in her ears until sleep took her.

Thunder boomed in the distance, waking Selest with a start. Snores echoed in the corridor. She dared a glimpse out the lattice window, noticing nothing but endless darkness. A figure darker still stirred in the corner. She gasped in horror. A faceless void gaped from beneath its hood, wreathed in shadows.

Selest slammed her back against the stone wall, petrified. The figure rose and crept toward her. Closer...closer. It removed its hood, revealing Thrion, his gray eyes filled with worry.

He knelt beside her.

"I thought you were," she grasped her side, "a Shadower." Her heart raced in her frozen body.

Thrion placed a hand on her shoulder, steadying her. "You're safe. No harm will come to you. It's all right."

"I can still feel the blade's cold cut." She peered out the window. "I still envision their faces in the blackness. I can't escape them—"

Thrion wrapped Selest's cloak around her. "It's all right. You're safe."

"What will happen when we leave the keeper's realm? I fear the dangers that await us."

"I don't know, Selest," he sighed. "I fear the same."

Selest grasped her pocket, tracing the Key's intricate design with her fingers. "Asteral, give us strength," she whispered. "I can't fathom how to press beyond my limits. I just want to stay here, in good faekeeper's company with no cares in the world."

Thrion furrowed his brow. "I'm deeply sorry, lass. I wish things were different, regardless of how much I know that we can't alter."

"I know. But I've been praying for you, Thrion," said Selest. "I hate that you still blame yourself."

Thrion squeezed her arm. "I'll be fine. It's just as Faern's dam told him— it takes time to mend a broken heart."

Thrion retreated back to his corner. "Get some shut-eye. We leave at dawn's first light."

Selest closed her eyes once more and drifted off, this time thankfully to a quiet, peaceful sleep.

The next morning when everyone woke they ate a quick breakfast. "I would like to grant you one of my Sapphirlings as a guide," announced Etris. "It will lead you past Lonely Valley and through the village of Crestford. Once you are on the Golden Sea's edge, my fae will depart and return to me."

Faern nodded. "I deem your forests quite hard to maneuver with the tricks of enchanted spells of the faes."

She nodded. "Be at peace, centaur. As long as you have a guide, you shall stay on course."

At that moment, a small wisp appeared, gleaming pale in the waxing sunlight. "Lead them through a safe passage to the edge of Orai," Etris instructed.

The sapphirling blinked in acknowledgment. The faekeeper turned to them.

"My fae shall lead you east of here. There, you shall find the Dimlit Road. Once you find it, do not stray from it. The Emeralding and Saphirling faes will try to lure you off the path, but my Sapphirling will shine brighter than all the rest, so that way you will be sure not to lose sight of it. But if you do, you will stray from the road, and it will be harder to navigate the valley. If you continue on the course, the path should lead you to the village of Crestford. Be wary of those who reside beyond, for their hearts are full of lust and greed."

A shiver ran down Selest's spine. She knew this part of the journey would prove treacherous, but hearing it aloud confirmed this part all the more dreadful.

Before they departed, they said their final farewells.

"May your road ahead be safe and your steed swift," said Etris.

"Thank you for providing us shelter for the night," said Faern, bowing in centaur fashion. "We are forever in your debt."

Etris returned the gesture. "As I am in yours."

Selest turned to look upon the grave for a final time, saying a silent goodbye.

The keeper stood at the threshold, watching the travelers take their leave under the veil of morning entwined in the wisp's blue light.

Chapter 15

The trees stood like guardians watching over the solitude of the forest. The boughs were lit by the blue fae light twinkling like stars against the mossy forest bed.

The wisp darted to and fro like a shooting star. One moment it was upon a gray rock, the next it was in a bed of clover.

They discovered the path stretched out like a gray thread. As they followed it, they noticed the trees finally gave way to a small glen leading into a valley. The deeper they ventured, the dimmer the lighting grew. The floral lights of faeries glimmered and glinted like sapphires.

The company peered in wonder at the earthen galaxy shimmering before them. They saw colors of peridot, emerald, and olive.

"It's like walking in a dream," Selest said, eyes wide. She recalled the stories she read that spoke of merrier times when centaurs and fae danced to reed pipe unseen.

They advanced in the midst of the starry spectacle. The fae was but a stone's throw away and it seemed that if one were to observe steadily one sphere, one could catch a glimpse of a slender angelic being embodied as a blue light. Soon, they approached a slight rise that marked the entrance to the Glenway.

Selest inhaled the chilling scent of pine as it pierced her lungs in arctic blasts. It reminded her of Starry Eve when the stars gleamed so bright it seemed you could reach out and touch them, and not even the vastness which lay between them could prevent her from doing so.

"How far along are we?" asked Thrion.

Faern glanced at his map. "We've got five more miles to travel before we reach the valley's end."

"We'll be outta there by nightfall," said Adair. "Good timing."

"I fear that doesn't prove true at the moment," Thrion said in a panicked tone. Selest peered into the sea of fae lights. The color drained from her face.

"What do you mean?" asked Adair.

"I mean that amidst our musings we've lost our guide."

Selest's heart quickened.

Suddenly, a reedy whisper echoed through the narrow domains.

Tra-la-lay
Alone, astray
Fa-la-lay
Dawn, day
La-le-lay
Follow, Fae

"Alay, Astray, Ere day, Unlay, Follow Fae…"

They found themselves in a thick cloak of mist. Selest glanced down. To her horror, the gray path had been replaced with green foliage.

North could be north, and yet south could be west at this rate, she thought.

"Stay close," said Faern. "We cannot risk getting separated."

They formed a tight ring, scanning the area. Almost instantaneously lights flickered in and out, in and out as a synchronized pulse.

Shades of green, intermixed with deep hues of sapphire, gleamed all around them.

The fading of the evening descended upon the green valley. The entire glen was lit in blue and green shadows revealing the high slopes of the valley.

Selest peered skyward and saw the narrowest sliver of dimly lit sky. There, she spotted the first light of a star—Asteral's Remnant. She lowered her gaze.

"Over there," she pointed. "I see a plume of smoke. It's just o'er the rise."

Faern followed her finger. "Good eye. Perhaps there we can ask for directions." He glanced at his map.

The centaur led them down a slope and up the steep rise. The mist that enshrouded them gave way as they crested the knoll.

The smell from a previous rainfall weighed down their chests and dampened their spirits.

They spotted the silhouette of a pub, its windows staring at them like two orange eyes.

Gray smoke plumes rose from a chimney in the waning light. At that moment, an eeriness engulfed them.

Slowly, they inched forward. "Be wary," said Thrion. "We don't need to attract any attention."

"This place gives off a rather strange atmosphere, doncha think?" Adair asked.

"Quite. Even from a distance, it seems." Selest shivered, hesitant to proceed.

"I'll wait out here," she said. "It shouldn't take that long, surely."

"We can't risk gettin' separated, lass. Best we stick together."

She sighed. "I've ne'er been in a pub before," she admitted. *My conscience tells me not to enter.* A sinful place it was. "Are you sure?"

"Just stick close, and you'll be all right. We won't let anything happen to you," reassured Thrion.

The closer they got to the pub, the more her heart quickened.

From the open door, the faint strum of a lute echoed. The sound was followed by the rich whistle of a shawm. Merry voices found their tune and hummed a rousing pub song.

Thrion led the pony to a rack nearby and tied its reins to the pole. They all went inside.

The strong scent of stale ale and mead was accompanied by the smell of fresh game. Most of those gathered were fauns of the forest, dwarves of the northern mountains, and men clad in the black of Shadenfell all seated at dimly lit oaken tables.

They were all drunk and jested in merriment. Many danced atop the tables with tankards in hand.

The company discerned fragments of a song—a light-hearted tune accompanied by lute and shawm.

Hi-ho
The diddly-o
O'er down we go
Down from the field and fen
Fro glade and glen
To the White Owl
Outside the winds howl
But in here the hearth is ablaze
Here we gaze in
Out into the cold
Where travelers pass by so bold
Into the pub built on birch and stone
Ale runs as plenty as a river
The beer-riddled wits are delivered
Older the wine
In its fine
Prime
Where riddle and rhyme
Will get ye a clean shave
Ere kin even forgave

An ax and spear to the head
As fine as wine crimson blood they bled
Three cheers for the dead
A bottle o' ale at his stead
Hi-ho, diddly-o
The fiddly-o
O'er up we go
To and fro
'Bove the White Mountains
Where wine runs as fountains
Hey-ho, Derry-o
Diddly-a
Fiddly-hey
Spindly-o!
O'er the Forest we go!
Hey!

After a few "pardon me's" and "watch it's," Thrion spotted an open table on the far right, and they approached the seats at the far corner.

Seating themselves, they observed the others.

Nearby, Shaden men eyed them suspiciously.

"I don't like the looks of those fell men one bit." Adair fingered the hilt of his dagger.

Selest felt their eyes on her. She pulled her cloak tighter around her wings as she caught bits of their conversation.

"...riding on the Dimlit Road, and we were ambushed by these— devils—cloaked in darkness, it seemed. Their mounts were horrid-lookin' beasts with blood-red eyes that'd make any man wish he were dead."

"What business ya think they've got?"

The man shivered. "Their business is their own. Some sort of artifact." He lowered his voice to a whisper. "Legend has it they've been seeking some sorta trinket to return to their master—to imprison him, and seek vengeance on some god that wronged 'em."

She felt the color drain from her face, grasping her pocket. *The Shadowers were tracking them?*

Adair leaned forward, his voice low. "We need to leave this place at once if our enemy is nigh."

"First we need to find the path. We can't leave and search for the trail in vain," said Thrion.

"Look around. We're surrounded by drunken fools. Ye think any of them would have any wits to help us?"

Thrion rose. "I'll go ask the barkeeper if he knows anyone." He turned to leave.

Faern grabbed his arm. "Be wary. Those Shaden hunters are suspicious of us."

He nodded and disappeared into the crowd.

Faern withdrew the map and studied it further.

Adair's fingers itched upon the hilt of his dagger.

Selest observed the Shaden hunters. Relief flooded over her when she found their eyes were no longer upon them. They had found a new victim, she realized, watching them approach a dark-skinned faun strumming a lyre.

They grabbed his lyre and tossed it around. The faun thrashed out in vain to fetch his instrument, but it was no use.

One hunter tripped him. The faun crashed into a table. The men roared with laughter.

"Why would they treat the poor faun like that?" she asked.

"It's a tavern filled with drunken ninnies. It's only normal behavior," Adair growled.

"That doesn't make it right." Selest rose from her seat.

"Stay!" said Faern in a firm tone. "Don't forget why we're here. We don't need to meddle in any disagreements that aren't ours."

"But no one else is going to help him—"

"Lass," warned Adair, "we must focus on the task at hand."

Selest hesitated. She peered back at the faun. The ruffians were spitting ale at him and strumming his lyre mockingly.

She rose from her seat and dashed to the faun.

"Selest!"

Hot fear shot up her spine as she passed the men and knelt beside the faun.

"Are you all right?" she asked. His brown eyes peered at her in shock.

"Told ya they were an odd lot," said the deep voice of a man.

Selest tensed, looking over her shoulder as three burly men towered above her.

"Ye think you can waltz in here and ruin our fun, missy?"

"N-now, fellas, c'mon," the faun interjected. "She's not from around these parts, she didn't know what she was doing—" One of the men kicked the faun in the leg.

"No!" Selest rose, standing between the men and the faun.

Selest dared a glimpse, noticing their malicious eyes sparking deviously.

"L-leave him alone," she said, voice trembling. "He did you no wrong."

A gruff hand grabbed her by the wrist and slammed her against the wall. She felt her wings crush on impact. With her free hand, she gouged at her assailant's eyes.

The man howled in pain. "Blasted witch!"

The other hunter raised his fist when an iron grip snapped at his hand. The man howled in pain.

"I wouldn't do that if I were you." Relief flooded over her as she recognized the familiar voice of Thrion.

The man with the lyre threw a punch. Thrion blocked his blow with his iron gauntlet, sending him toppling over a table where a band of dwarves sat. Mugs of ale spilled all over them.

They gave a cry of fury and began throwing punches. It wasn't long until the whole tavern was in an uproar.

Thrion guided Selest out amidst the brawl, shielding her from the chaos. "We need to leave. Now," he spoke in a firm tone.

They rushed out of the tavern and into the shelter of the trees. Selest hunched over gasping for breath. She stared at the ground bathed in the pale moonlight, trying to avoid Adair's gaze. Yet even in the waning light she could still feel the blaze of the dwarf's anger.

"What were ye thinkin'?" he demanded.

"I—," a lump formed in her throat, "did what I thought was right."

"By nearly getting yerself beaten to death?" yelled the dwarf. She wanted to shrink—shrink until she felt invisible. "Don't forget our purpose. Ye need to focus."

Absent-mindedly, she nodded. Deep guilt weighed on her chest. *I did what I deemed right, didn't I? Wasn't that all that mattered?*

Hot tears streamed down her face. She squeezed her eyes shut.

"I'm sorry," she blurted, peering at each of them in turn. "I saw someone in danger, and I wanted to help them."

Faern towered before her. Shame tugged at her chest. She bowed her head. "Faern, I—"

The centaur placed a hand on her shoulder. "What's done is done."

Adair began to protest. "Centaur! Ye can't be serious—"

He raised his hand in the air. Adair went silent.

Faern knelt at her height. "You could've been badly injured, dear heart. I know your intentions were good, but now you must realize that your actions have consequences. As of now, I suspect those hunters will be keeping a close eye on us."

Selest nodded.

Turning to Thrion, Faern asked, "What did you find out?"

Thrion sighed. "The barkeeper said the path is half a mile from here. I deem it best we travel away from the road, knowing our pursuers are after us."

Peering into the blackness, Selest shivered.

"We just need a way to make sure we don't get swayed by the fae's enchantment," said Thrion. "We need a guide."

At that moment, they heard a twig snap.

They jerked their heads at the sound and saw the faun limping toward them.

She rushed over to his side. "Are you all right, Mr. Faun?"

He was startled. "There ya are. I ought to thank you for saving my skin back there.

Are you hurt?"

"Ah. Just a bad limp. I've dealt with worse." He paused, looking at the group, then he said abruptly, "I'm Oskari, minstrel extraordinaire. But just Oskar's fine." The faun cleared his throat.

She nodded. "I'm Selest." She turned to her friends, introducing them.

"A pleasure." The faun dusted off his instrument.

"I thought one of the men stole your lyre," she said.

"Nay, he was too distracted with the fight." His brown eyes twinkled to a rhythmic tune of the strumming of his lyre. His curly brown hair seemed to dance to his tune as well.

"We need to figure out how to lure the faes away from the Dimlit Road so we can stay our course and—" Faern began, eyeing him skeptically. "You, Master Faun, you wouldn't know how to lure the fae away would you?"

Oskar peered in awe at the mighty centaur. "With just a strum of my lyre, I guarantee the faes shall part." Quickly, he added, "T-they're fond of love music—"

"We don't expect this jester to be our guide, do we?" Adair interrupted, crossing his arms.

"What other guide do we have?" asked Thrion.

Adair sighed. "Very well."

Adair fetched the pony and they all turned toward the road, leaving the pub brawl in full swing behind them.

Oskari began to lead the way strumming his lyre. With each vibration, the faes dispersed. Soon, they found the silver road lit by a pale waxing gibbous as the faes swirled about like pieces of colorful stained glass.

Chapter 16

All night they followed the gloomy road. Morning dawned bright and fair when they spotted a town in the distance.

The company trudged on in silence, attuned to every creak and every crack of twig and leaf.

The dawning sun cast rays of bright light, warding off the shade.

Gradually, the trees thickened and towered above them like ancient pillars. The mossy foliage formed a luscious carpet of rich green. Mushrooms grew as white as pearls unveiled by gem light. The path swerved this way and that, around trees, and under boughs. All shone with a bold hue. The enchantment of all the forest was in Rein; it was the very heart of the land. The travelers heard the rustling breeze plucking the strings of ivy among the noble trees. The melodious sound blended with another sound that caught their attention.

They climbed a steep knoll where the trees receded into a clearing. The farther they went, the stronger Selest heard the rush of a waterfall.

The sound brought with it a scent of fragrant refreshment.

Breathing in, they could declare they breathed the whole of the forest. It had such a sweetness to it, like rainwater falling upon the mists of a rainbow.

Silver rocks lay scattered before them. They found themselves making quite a steep ascent; the higher they went the scent became almost tangible.

Finally, they peered upon the majestic sight. The waters fell as pearlescent curtains into a deep pool upon a sheer cliff of the same silver rock. The waterfall drowned out all other sources of sound as the company neared the towering monstrosity. It made Selest feel small and hushed. It demanded her full attention as the spray dampened her outer and inner essence.

Oskar swept his hand. "Welcome to Eas Diamant, the crown jewel of Crestford."

Selest's eyes widened as she beheld the sunlight flicking its golden rays playfully upon the white rushing water.

"It's wonderful." A smile broke out across her face.

She spread her wings underneath her cloak, letting the waterfall's mist envelop her.

Her staff felt like ice thawing in the warm spray.

"Selest, come!" yelled Adair. Reluctantly she followed, the others trailing behind.

"So, Oskar, what's your connection with Crestford?" Thrion asked.

"Well," the faun explained with excitement glinting in his eyes, "I'm originally from Brandemere, but I've been a wandering bard playing hither and thither. I've performed up there. The Crestford crowd is similar to the lads back at White Owl Inn."

Selest shivered. "I don't like the sound of that."

The group continued following the golden stream fed by the waterfall for some time until they halted beside a still pool of water that glistened in the sun's rays.

"It's similar to the Mirror of Crysil's," thought Selest.

Then she asked, "What's the significance of this pool?"

The faun peered at the landmark, eyes twinkling. "Ah yes, the pool. Why this was the Mirror of Na Brach. It belonged to Father Summer."

Selest peered north. The village of Crestford lay nestled between two faces of mossy stone a quarter mile away, yet she could discern a tall stony arch adorned with green moss between them.

She glanced behind her to where the waterfall was now lost within the hills, though the faint rush still confirmed its presence.

She exhaled a sigh of relief as they made the final trek to the walled town.

The closer they got the more the arch loomed above them until they were engulfed by its shadow.

They circled the mossy wall, halting before an imposing gate. Six bars of thick brass guarded the entrance.

Selest peered between the bars. She observed cobblestone streets leading to white clay houses adorned with moss. Glass jars were strewn between houses, containing fae lights of green and blue.

The faun gave a huff of displeasure. "I don't understand. They always have their doors open at this early hour."

Faern pranced uneasily. "There's an unsettling air about this place."

"Aye." The dwarf sniffed the air. "A foul reek is about."

Selest scrunched her nose. A rotting odor roused her senses.

HHHhhhhhhhh...

She froze to her very core.

The horse stirred uneasily.

"What was that?" Oskari asked.

"An old foe," said Thrion, unsheathing his sword. The others did the same.

The company turned around. Beyond the morning mist, they noticed a tall, morbid figure. Its red eyes penetrated Selest's soul.

Thought soon became reality as the one morphed into eleven.

Selest shrank behind the others, clutching at her staff with a white-knuckled grip. Her heart pounded with sheer ferocity.

"Everyone, grab a torch from the wall!" Thrion commanded.

As they did so, the Eleven advanced.

"Selest," Thrion gestured, "open the gate."

She nodded, pressing her back against the gate, shaking.

Selest turned and slipped the Key from her pocket.

With trembling hands, she poked and prodded for it to fit the keyhole. To her relief, she heard a faint *click!*

Quickly, she shoved the Key back into her pocket. She grasped at the cool brass of the gate and pushed all her weight onto it. It did not budge.

"Help me!" she yelled. The faun rushed to her aid.

Faern appeared at her side. Together, they pushed until the gate finally creaked open.

"Come on, get in! Hurry!" Faern yelled.

"C'mon!" Oskar grabbed hold of Selest's hand and led the way inside. The pony followed quickly without prodding.

They looked in horror as the others fought the enemy.

Thrion charged a kelpie, piercing its skull with savage force. The mount reared, its rider falling to the ground. Selest was certain she could see vengeance burning in the Shadower's black eyes. With a shrill whistle, the beast charged at his persecutor. The Shadowers followed.

Adair rushed to Thrion's side. He gave a battle cry, waving his torch in a deadly circle, warding off the enemy.

"Come on!" Faern yelled. Thrion and Adair sprinted for the gate, their pursuers close behind.

"Hurry!" shouted Selest. They grew closer—closer.

The two rushed inside.

Faern reared, swinging his torch in a vengeful arc. The deadly flame cut through the faceless Shadowers.

He raised his sword and sliced the kelpie's neck as he grasped the gate.

Life dimmed from the gaping eyes. The odor was stronger than ever.

"Get in, quickly!" shouted Thrion.

"Faern, watch out!" Selest cried.

A blade sliced the centaur's belly.

"Agh!" The mighty warrior gave a cry of pain.

He released his grip on the gate. Thrion planted his hand between brass and stone. With all his strength, he held the door open.

"Take my hand!" yelled Adair.

Faern grabbed the dwarf's hand. He yanked the centaur through the opening.

The gate slammed shut.

Selest heard a sickening *crunch*.

Faern howled in pain, his leg caught. Adair pushed the gate back open. "Can ye move yer leg lad?"

"No," hissed Faern through gritted teeth.

Oskar rushed over, tenderly removing the centaur's leg from between stone and brass.

A Shadower raised his sword above his head.

Thrion threw his torch. The flame engulfed the monster's face. It dropped its sword as it gave a bone-chilling shriek.

The gate clanged shut.

The Shadowers screeched with fury, pacing in front of the gate.

Selest turned from the horrid scene, examining the town before her.

All was quiet. The only sound was footsteps approaching from a stairwell of the tower of the fortified wall.

Adair rushed to the centaur's aid, his expression grave.

Suddenly, they found themselves surrounded by guards, spears pointed at them.

"Who goes there?" a gruff voice resounded. The guard was adorned with an emerald aketon with golden trim. He wore a cervelliere on his head.

"My friend is injured," replied Thrion, nursing his hand. "Could you help us? We're being pursued."

"Ye lured the Cloaked Riders." The lanky man stared at them, a crazed glint in his eyes. "'Sides, how'd ya open the gate anyways?"

Oskari approached the guard. "Caz! It's me, Oskar! I came to the White Unicorn many times to play a jig or two."

The old geezer wasn't yet convinced. "That still doesn't explain how ya opened the gate—" The bloody cries of the enemy resounded from beyond the fortress.

Selest's heart pounded so hard she thought it would rip out of her chest.

Thrion stepped forward. "Never mind that now. We need aid. You have not us to fear, but the very enemy who has come to pursue us."

Caz hesitated as a crowd began to grow.

"Let 'em pass thro' 'ere. They mean no harm," said a voice.

"They've put us all in danger," argued another in protest.

Selest held her breath.

After a moment of silence, Old Caz replied, "Go to my brother at Conan's Mercantile if aid is what ya need. I'm sure he'll offer ya shelter for the night."

He turned to a fellow guard. "Sound the alarm to secure the perimeter."

Five short blasts followed.

Caz turned to them. "Go. Yer safe for now, at least until word spreads about what ya lured here."

They aided Faern as they followed the faun to Conan's Mercantile.

Selest felt the cool breeze whip across her face as she strained to keep a steady hold of Faern.

His wound oozed blood and sweat as he panted heavily.

Just when her legs were about to give out, the faun seized to a halt.

They were at a small cottage near part of the circular wall. It was quiet.

Above the oaken door read a sign: *Conan's Merch.*

Oskar knocked on the door. No one answered.

Thrion turned to Selest, nodding.

She unlocked the door, and the faun held it open as they aided the centaur inside.

The shop had shelves and trays on tables stocked with many trinkets. The trays were filled with colorful beads, silks and satins, and fine articles of clothing. Books lined the shelves ringing the perimeter. The books were old and looked like they held many secrets. Other shelves were stocked with pots and pans, dishes, and silverware. And yet others held baubles like antiques and decorations. On the far west wall, there were also weapons and wear for war and hunting.

They made their way to a back room where the mighty centaur collapsed to the floor, panting laboriously.

"Faern!" Selest rushed to the centaur's side.

He grasped at his stomach, writhing in pain.

Faern heaved a painful sigh that was almost a whimper.

Adair retrieved his medicine bag from around his shoulder and dug through it.

His brow creased in grave dismay. "I've run low on Evenmint." He lowered his gaze.

Thrion turned to Adair. "Surely there's some in this shop. I'll see what I can find." He began rummaging through the medicinal display.

Selest followed, looking at the labels.

Thyme—chamomile—woad—

The Mint wasn't there. Thrion tossed more jars aside. Still none.

Selest glanced above him. A label read *Red Remedy.* "There! Is that it?" She pointed to a bottle of a red substance.

Thrion followed her gaze. "It is."

"I found a bottle o' water." Oskar hurried to their aid. "It's been settin' for days, though."

"It'll do." Adair accepted the water. Thrion tore a piece of his cloak, dousing it with water.

He applied it to the cut.

Faern writhed in pain.

Selest wrapped her thin arm around him, caressing his back. "Sure, it's all right. It's all right." A lump formed in her throat. "It's all right."

Selest said a silent prayer. *Asteral, please, heal him, please.*

Suddenly, a creak of the door echoed throughout the small mercantile. Everyone's gaze shifted in alarm at the entrance.

The footsteps sounded faint at first, but then grew closer to the back room where they were hiding. Thrion rose from behind a shelf of books and approached the door.

He fingered his sword, waiting.

After a moment of feet shuffling about, the footsteps were closer than ever.

Thrion receded into the shadows. The knob rattled as it turned. The wooden door opened, revealing an old merchant.

He was a pitiful sight. He was as thin as a reed and scrawny as a starved street cat. His clothes and apron were stained and in tatters, though they did complement his scraggly gray hair.

The worn merchant gawked in shock at the group.

"Conan," Oskar exclaimed.

The man was paralyzed with fear.

"My sincerest apologies for the inconvenience. We're dreadfully sorry for intruding on your home. Ol' Caz said you could help us—" Oskar pleaded.

The old man's jaw snapped open and shut, eyes wide. "Linens and lemons—" The old man fainted on the floor.

Selest rushed to his side and checked his pulse. It was weak, but beating nonetheless.

"Oi!" Oskar rushed to them. "I'll take care o' the ol' geezer from here."

Selest gazed at Conan with pity and turned to her friends.

Adair bandaged Faern's stomach, while Thrion stood by the window, nursing his wounded hand.

"Thrion, are you all right?" Selest winced, noticing the palm of his hand was bruised and swollen. She turned to the dwarf. "Adair, we need your aid."

"I'll be there in a moment!" he yelled over his shoulder. Shortly after, the dwarf approached them, examining the hunter's wound.

"I think it's fractured," Thrion strained to say.

"Aye, the blood vessels in your hand are damaged. Luckily, ya still feel pain, meaning yer nerves aren't damaged. Ye need ice to reduce the swelling."

Adair turned to Selest. "Lass, fetch me some ice from the cellar and some cloth."

Shortly after, she returned with a block of ice and a white cloth.

Adair accepted it and wrapped the ice in the cloth before applying it to Thrion's wound.

He winced. Selest knelt beside Thrion, placing a comforting hand on his shoulder. "Shhh. It's all right." She didn't know how long it was before she found herself resting against the stone wall nearby.

Early the next morning, she found herself lying on the floor wrapped in a dark cloak. Yawning, she blinked at the setting moonlight filtering through the lattice window. Wearily she rose, hearing voices from around the corner. She stumbled after the sound. She found Conan and the others seated at a table with a meal of oatmeal and berries.

"...we've twenty miles to go before we reach Orai," said a deep voice, "yet we're trapped."

"Yes. The men of Crestford have scouted the perimeter. Those fiends have been circling the fortress all night."

"They won't rest until we're dead," muttered Adair. "It won't be long until they find a way to breach the entrance."

"Caz, can't yer men ward off those demons?"

"Nay. No matter what we do, they're unstoppable. Our men are unskilled to handle such devilish monstrosities."

Selest startled as a floorboard creaked beneath her. They all turned to her. She peered at them, eyes wide.

"Come 'ere, lass," said Caz. "Didn't mean to frighten ya. Come, eat."

She found a seat next to Caz and Oskar.

Adair sighed. "Thrion and Faern are gravely injured. Even if we did manage to escape, there's no way we could cover twenty miles alone."

Five short horn blasts rang out.

Everyone froze.

Oskar shook his head. "This is bad. This is really bad."

Suddenly, a loud knock sounded on the door. "Sir, the gate has been breached! The enemy has broken in!"

Selest's heart dropped. "What do we do?" She prayed to Asteral above.

She felt the guard's eyes linger on the company, his glare screaming accusation.

"They're the ones who lured 'em here. 'Tis their doin'."

Oskar lowered his head. "It's not our intent to bring danger upon this village, Caz, you know that."

"Intentions do not matter. Leave this place, and lead 'em off, since it's you they want!" shouted the guard, pointing his spear at them. "It's because of ye we're in this mess in the first place."

"Silence!" Faern's voice boomed like thunder reverberating against Selest's chest. He lowered his voice. "*You* listen to *me*. These fiends have been on our tail for days. One of our own was nearly killed."

Selest winced, the blade of Emberthel flashing in her mind's eye. "*They're* responsible for all the pain and destruction," continued Faern. "We've done nothing but escape them. They've chosen to follow us. We barely got away with our lives—fighting and straining to survive. Evil has stirred for many years in the far West, and we've been driven from our very homes."

The guard hesitated.

"He's right," said Thrion. "We're some of the few survivors that have barely escaped with our lives. This is not just our enemy, but yours as well. And we don't stand a chance against them. Our only hope is to throw aside our grievances and work together."

The guard set his jaw. "The people of the West were blind—too blind to prevent the coming spread of evil."

Selest sighed. The events of Starry Eve and the wizard weighed heavy on her mind.

"You're right. My people were blind. They wouldn't listen—"

"Lass," Adair said in a gentle but firm tone.

"But blaming the past will solve nothing. The only thing that matters is what we do now," Selest said, shaking off the memories.

"If ye mean what yer sayin', then it's you all they want," said Caz. "Make yerselves known to them, and they'll leave us be—it'd be best for all of us—'fore they tear this whole village apart stone by stone."

"They'll do no such thing!" exclaimed Conan.

"Traitor!" yelled Caz. Without warning, the old guard sprinted forward, grabbing Selest by the arm.

She was yanked from where she sat, the movement causing everyone to draw their weapons.

"Don't touch her!" Thrion yelled.

Selest felt the tickle of cold metal as Caz pointed the spear's tip against her neck.

She gritted her teeth, a stinging needle of betrayal piercing her chest. "Let go of me."

Caz pressed the spear tighter. "Lower yer weapons—else you'll be sorry," he said.

Selest saw the fear in their eyes. She knew she'd have to save herself.

The guard inched toward the door. "Stay where ya are!" he yelled.

She felt something wet trickle down her skin. She tensed, paralyzed with fear. Before she could react, she found herself outside in the blinding dawn. Nightmarish cries rang out beyond the rooftops, making her blood run cold. Her vision blurred in a kaleidoscope of tears as she struggled to break free.

"Hey!" shouted Caz, "over here!"

Hooves echoed against the cobblestone.

Every fiber in her body screamed.

"NO!" She raised her foot and drove her heel into the man's foot. He seized his foot, howling in pain.

Selest shoved him to the ground and dashed for the mercantile.

A shadow engulfed her, darker than night itself. She could feel its red eyes burning her back.

Footsteps thundered from behind.

Closer—closer—

Thrion shot an arrow from the doorway; she felt it zip past her. A pitiful shriek ripped through the air.

She turned and slammed herself into Thrion's arms.

She felt her lungs explode as she gasped for air.

"Are you hurt?" asked Adair, examining her.

She grasped her neck, shaking. "What are we going to do? We're tra—"

A crash shattered the air. Selest turned. The Shadower loomed above them.

Thrion pierced the enemy's head with an arrow. It gave a blood-curdling scream.

"Everyone, to me!" Thrion shouted.

Selest rushed behind him.

Thrion kicked the bookshelf. It crashed into the hallway.

"What the blazes are ya doin'?" Adair roared. "We'll be cornered."

"Dwarf's right. What're ya thinkin'?" Oskar exclaimed.

Conan rushed to the table. He fetched a candle. "Burn in Hell, ya devils!" He lit the bookshelf aflame. The nascent blaze licked greedily at wood and parchment. The flame wouldn't cease until its appetite was satisfied.

Conan opened the back door. "Go!"

Immediately the others rushed outside. The village buildings gleamed like skeletons in the waxing sunlight.

As they skirted the city wall, the silhouetted trees stood like wooden pillars peering at them with shady eyes.

Selest viewed a now dimmed sky, with faint pinholes amid black leaves. The stars twinkled slowly like a pendulum ticking off the minutes of certain doom.

A horn sounded. "Caz," whispered Selest.

"Run!" shouted Thrion, grabbing her hand.

Blindly, she strained to match Thrion's long strides. The torches from the wall flickered playfully against vacant windows as they sped past. She glanced back. From afar, she was certain she caught a shadow darker than night.

She gasped. "Thrion—"

"Don't—look back—"

Finally, the wall's side door came into view. Their pony stood before it as if it knew this was the exit they needed. They halted abruptly. Faern collapsed to the ground, grasping at his hoof.

Immediately, Selest fetched the Key, squinting. She felt for the keyhole. Her heart quickened. "I can't find it."

Adair brought a torch closer.

To her relief, the keyhole was in sight. Selest unlocked the door.

She burst into the forest, panting.

A bloodcurdling scream ripped through the air.

Someone crashed to the ground. The door slammed shut.

Sobs tore through the air. "What have I done? Woe is me! I am undone!" It was the frail voice of Conan.

Selest rushed to the old man. "Conan, are you—?"

"Stay, he's mad," warned Adair.

She stopped in her tracks.

The old man's gaze penetrated her core. "I'm so sorry, Asteral, forgive me. The Quest failed. The Key is lost to the enemy."

The color drained from her face. How did he know of the Quest?

"Asteral, forgive me, I failed, after all these years—I—"

He dropped to the ground, motionless.

Selest gasped.

The merchant was dead.

The company stood in shock over his body.

Thrion roused them. "Come. We must hasten to the Council. 'Tis a day's journey from here. Faern is injured, and we don't have much time. I pray we'll meet others arriving at the Council to aid us for the remainder of the way."

Thrion led the way.

Without another word, they disappeared silently into the forest. As Selest dared a glance back, the last thing she saw was hellfire above a forsaken town.

Chapter 17

All day they traveled southeast hoping and praying their pursuers weren't nigh.

As they hurried their weary and injured bodies on foot, it wasn't until mid-morning that they reached the end of the Enchanted Forest.

Before them, a golden sea stretched as far as they could see.

Selest held her breath. Was it real, or was it all a dream? She thought back to the events of the last day; how did Conan know about the Quest?

She pondered the scene before her. They had spent most of their recent days in grave peril. Now, they were on the edge of paradise.

She scoffed. 'Twas too good to be true.

As they trudged through the golden prairie, the sun peaked upon the blue dome.

Occasionally, they caught glimpses of farmsteads in the distance.

The flatland around them gradually ascended. They were soon surrounded by swells upon swells of hills.

As they climbed a steep grade, she quickened her pace, the wind pushing her to reach the top.

Selest's calves tightened, her knees buckling beneath her when they finally conquered the ascent.

And lo! the White House of Orla stood before them as a pearl nestled in the Golden Sea.

To her right, she spotted specks of red and brown.

"What is down there?" Selest squinted.

Faern observed the plains below, eyes sharp as a hawk. "Centaurs of the Starry Plains—my kin."

Adair fingered the hilt of his dagger. "Are they friend or foe?"

"Friend," replied Faern.

As the herd grew closer, they descended the steep hill.

Selest was certain the centaurs spotted them as they drew closer. The formidable creatures formed a ring around the company, towering above them.

She held her breath.

The first centaur she had ever seen was Faern, but now she was surrounded by an entire host, each greater than Faern in stature.

The description from her books of lore did not do justice in describing these beings.

They were slim and well-fit for battle. Their sleek coats were of various shades of red and brown, but not the golden brown of Faern's coat. Their skin was dark and tan.

They were armed with bows and arrows, fixed to shoot.

"Stay, stay!" Faern said.

The surrounding centaurs parted. A male stood before them.

He was the tallest and greatest centaur of them all. His coat was a dark bay, matching the color of his hair. About his bare muscular chest twin lances were slung.

He examined the company, arms crossed. "We have a brother amongst us."

His voice was deep and rich like freshly plowed soil.

Faern bowed in centaur fashion. "It's good to see one of my kin."

"Likewise." He peered past Faern. "What business do you have with the races of dwarf, faun, and man?"

"We're survivors from the West. Our homes have been taken by the evil that lurks foully in these lands."

"I can see your journey proved ill." Turning to two centaurs, he ordered, "Aid our brother the rest of the way."

They supported Faern with sturdy arms as they proceeded.

"Astria, come hither!" he said, and an auburn centauress emerged from the crowd.

"Go ahead of us, be swift, and tell them of our arrival."

"Yes, Chief." Bowing, she stole a glance at Faern, and her emerald eyes locked with his light-brown gaze before she galloped away.

The leader turned back to Faern. "I am Adhearn, Starwatcher, and Chief of Galielle. Pray tell, do you hail from Perisade?"

"I do."

Adhearn's expression was grave. "Do any remain?"

Faern sighed. "Not for a long time. After the Shadow War, many of my brothers and sisters fought and either died in battle or simply left Perisade. I was the only one who remained in my native land. Now, I've been driven from my home once more."

"Word has spread of the growing evil there."

"Indeed," replied Faern. "We've sought to reach the Council."

"'Tis good you survived. We'll need more representatives from the West."

Together, they neared the house. Selest let out a breath of relief. They had made it. After weeks of peril, they had finally reached their destination.

As they approached the marbled building, sentinels clad from head to toe in amber-gold armor stood guard before the arched entrance. Both guards were armed with one spear each pointed to the heavens, gleaming like two silver suns.

"Her Grace has been expecting your arrival."

As the Oraian guards parted, the pilgrims passed through the gate.

The thumping of a staff echoed in Selest's ears. She glanced at where the noise was. A hooded figure caught her attention.

Thrion trembled, stumbling to his knees. He bowed his head as if a wreath of red hot shame adorned it. "Father—"

The wizard embraced his son. "I prayed every day that you would arrive." Silent tears streamed down his face.

Thrion fiddled with the chain around his neck, the sapphire star gleaming in the noonday light.

Yaelas' gray eyes peered intently at the others. "I see you have acquired four companions." He glanced at Selest. "I see only one being from the Glade."

Thrion nodded. "I tried convincing the others, but it was too late." He turned away. "I've failed."

Selest placed a hand on his shoulder. "'Twas their own denial that blinded them. You can't hold yourself accountable for the actions of my people, Thrion. They made their choice." Her voice caught in her throat. "And I've made mine."

"She speaks the truth, son. You've made known the coming evil, as have I these three years past. 'Twas all you could've done." He cleared his throat. "Come. You've had a long journey, and you should settle in. But first, tell me your names."

The four briefly introduced themselves. "Ah, yes. Very good," said Yaelas. "Come then, I'll escort you in."

Yaelas led them to a marble courtyard. In the center flowed a fountain carved in the likeness of a three-pointed leaf. Surrounding it, winged folk fashioned in warm-colored robes were scattered here and there, either talking about their day or reading books of old lore.

By the fountain, they found Astria with a Virtue adorned in gold.

The Virtue, Orla, greeted them merrily. She had a bright aura that one couldn't help but notice. Her honey-blonde hair matched the sunny tone of her eyes that could light up any sorrowful heart.

Selest stood awestruck by her radiance. Her wings were arches of soft brown etched in a halo of gold. Even the Temptress's guise couldn't surpass that of the Goldess herself.

Orla greeted them with the utmost respect.

"Hail! Daughter of Daybringer." Yaelas bowed, followed by the rest.

"We've been expecting you, Company of the West. You have arrived early, as the council is nearly a month from now. In the meantime, make yourselves at home, and please do not hesitate to ask for anything."

Faern strained to bow. "We're humbled by your hospitality, my lady—" His legs buckled despite the centaurs' support.

Orla rushed forth. "Stay. You are injured."

Adair knelt beside him. "I fear the swelling in your hoof has traveled through your leg." The dwarf withdrew a nettle leaf, applying it to his wound. "After I treat the infection, it's best to take it easy. It'll take several weeks for yer injury to heal."

"My servants will show you to your rooms. Get some rest. Your journey proved perilous. Now, you can all take comfort. No harm shall come to you here."

She turned, gliding like a golden bird upon a string. Selest was certain her feet barely touched the floor. With a flick of her hand, servants approached.

Thrion turned to Selest. "I'll meet with you shortly," he said. "For now rest, and I'll fetch you afterward."

One old archangel led Selest to her room, walking her through the large estate. The servant escorted Selest beneath an awning supported by quartz pillars and into a white hallway. Finally, she found herself in an exquisitely furnished room. The sight of a bed made her heart faint in exhaustion.

"New clothes are on your bed," gestured the maid, "and a bath is also prepared for you if you'd like."

Selest turned to the maid. "How did Lady Orla prepare for our coming with such speed?"

The maid chuckled. "She doesn't hesitate to prepare for guests when an occasion such as this arises. It's her specialty. Her hospitality lights up any room and the heart of any servant."

Selest smiled. "I see." Observing the room with renewed interest she turned to the maid, who was bent and grayed with age.

"Thank you."

The maid bowed. "My pleasure."

Selest shut the door behind her.

Without much thought, she peeled off her armor and stripped off her clothes, soaking in the fresh basin of water, extending her wings awkwardly.

Later, she dressed in her new garments and stared at her reflection in a mirror, aghast.

The last time she had any of these comforts of home was at the Temptress's domain. She clutched her pocket. Empty. Almost on the verge of panic, Selest's heart stopped.

She raced to the bed, groping her pocket tunic until she felt the familiar outline.

She sighed with relief.

Thanks to Asteral, the Key is safe. She faced the mirror once more, Key in hand.

Pressing her hand against the glass, she watched as the sun glinted in the many facets of the Key. There, she pondered Conan's death as she combed through her silky blue hair.

Selest then turned and settled into bed, sighing at the comfort.

Half awake, yet half asleep, searing thoughts penetrated her mind like unwelcome guests.

She clutched the Key in her grasp.

Questions raced through her mind. How did Conan of all people know of the Quest? How did her father know Yaelas? Does he know what she possesses?

She shoved the Key into her dress pocket. She dare not dwell on it. But no matter how hard she tried, those thoughts haunted her.

A knock woke her. She stretched, yawning. Opening the door, she smiled to see Thrion. He was in new attire and was well-groomed, his hand freshly bandaged.

"How's your hand?" she asked.

He wiggled his fingers. "Stiff. After I exercise my hand for a few weeks, it should be good as new." He creased his brow. "What about you?"

She stretched. "Tired."

"I didn't mean to wake you, lass, but I came to tell you that my father desires to speak with us regarding our journey."

She nodded. "There are pressing questions I wish to address—if that is permitted."

"He'll answer them as best he can."

He beckoned her forward. "Come. They're anxious to see you."

She followed Thrion across a hallway. The blue-purple evening light graced the land as the candles burned softly in their sconces.

They approached a room located in a far corner of the hallway.

There, she found Adair examining Faern's freshly bandaged leg while Yaelas sat patiently observing the twilight's stars through the lattice window.

He was jolted from his thoughts when they approached.

"Come, gather round. There is much to discuss."

The company gave Yaelas a full account of their journey beginning when Thrion first met Selest, to the Shadowers ambushing them at Crestford.

At the mention of Conan, the wizard coughed abruptly.

Selest nearly rose from her seat. "You knew him, didn't you."

Thrion placed a hand on her shoulder. "All in good time."

Thrion turned to his father. Yet confusion was apparent in his voice as well. "Father, you didn't happen to know of the Key?"

Questions tumbled from Selest's mouth.

"How did you know my father? And how did he come to bear the Key... ?"

"Enough!" yelled Yaelas, trembling. A gloom gathered around his head like a dark halo.

"What do I not know?" Selest whispered.

Thrion quietly observed his father. "On the verge of the Shadow War all those years ago, you were as calm as a still stream, yet the very mention of the Key haunts you so."

The dark halo faded as Yaelas cleared his throat. "Forgive me, but the mention of the Key brings back memories that seem too dark to reminisce over. Alas! I deem it best if you all knew the truth, but I fear the pain it may cause."

He straightened himself in the chair and took a deep breath. "Sixteen years ago, I resided in the Misty Forest. I was the talk of The Glade as news of my wanderings reached them. So foresters would come from far and wide to my humble abode. There, I met a young hunter by the name of Savion. He told me he was hunting Shaden merchants clad in navy garments.

"He sought my help, telling me his betrothed was captured by these cruel merchants. He claimed she was going on a stroll when they fettered her in chains. So in exchange for saving my son from the hands of witches, I decided to assist him on his quest to rescue the archangel."

"D-did they capture her because of her wings?" asked Selest.

Yaelas sighed. "Yes. Alas, many traders captured young winged maidens to harvest and sell their wings."

She placed a hand over her mouth, the color draining from her face.

The witch in the guise of Crysil was right.

"But after Elarael, wife of the Autumn Virtue, was slain and her wings taken, other archangels began cutting off their wings during the Siege of the West, so how could my mother still have hers?"

Yaelas sighed yet again. "Upon reaching adulthood, they were given a choice. Most chose to surgically remove their wings, but your mother was among the few who kept hers. And it was a price Arisael was willing to pay. So we went. There we took the guise of Shadenfell men and rescued her from imprisonment. Alas, her wings were already taken.

"On our way back to Sovoria, we took a shortcut across the Peridot Mountains, for your mother was in dire need and was beyond my skill to heal. So we stopped in Crestford. A young guard named Caz said his brother was a merchant who had some skill in medicine. Savion was hesitant at first but later agreed. So Caz led us to him.

"There, Conan treated your mother and requested an herb from his storeroom. So I went to look for it."

He paused. "Amid trinkets and such, I discovered the Key of Ezelex. I confronted him, but he wanted nothing to do with it. I didn't want the Key to be in the possession of such a reckless person, so Conan let me take it.

"I knew the world was in mortal danger. So it was Líadan, the Virtue of Spring, Savion, Arisial, and I who strove to use the Key and lock the Devil into his prison so Asteral's will could be satisfied." Yaelas bowed his head as grief weighed upon him. "Alas, we were blind. My wife lost her life."

Thrion clenched his fists.

Yaelas continued. "After her death, I deemed it best if it went west to The Glade with Arisial, for I knew the time was not right. But I can see it now resides with you."

Selest met his eyes. "My mother died in childbirth. She gave it to my father, and before she died she told him to charge me to fulfill the Quest. This became known to me when the witches seized The Glade. I had no idea what he meant—until now."

Thrion's grief could no longer be contained. He rose, yelling. "You kept this from me—from us?" Tears streamed down his face. "Now you tell us? Of all times?"

Yaelas said nothing.

Thrion left the room, slamming the door behind him.

Unbearable silence cloaked them. The tranquil rush of the fountain lulled them into an ocean of deep thought.

"What must be done to ensure the success of this Quest?" Faern asked.

"Ye can't be serious," Adair said in a firm tone. "I came to this council to receive my homeland back."

"The West is lost," spoke Yaelas, "and so is the Central Region and beyond, lest we fulfill the Quest."

Selest clutched her pocket, a wave of grief and fury threatening to drown her.

"I deem it wise you present the Key on the day of the Council, for this matter concerns all."

Selest placed a hand on her chest. "F-forgive me. This is a-a lot to take in. I think I-I'll excuse myself."

She rushed out of the room.

"Selest!" Adair called after her. She paid no heed. She dashed to her room, slamming the door behind her.

Her whole life was a lie.

She grasped her wings, grabbing handfuls of feathers and ripping them asunder.

She sobbed. She grasped the root of her wing and began twisting with all her might. Fresh pain coursed down her back.

A glint of steel caught her eye. She stopped. Blindly, she rushed forward and seized the dagger from its hilt.

Her hand trembled as she grasped her wing. She sawed at the root, clenching her teeth.

She sobbed until the pain exploded throughout her entire back.

The blade slipped from her hand, clanging to the floor. Her knees burned as they slammed into the hard marble tile.

A red line blurred her vision. She toppled over and knew no more.

Chapter 18

Dawn reluctantly revealed its head as Selest opened her eyes. She observed the prairie painted in golden sunlight.

Fresh pain washed over her. She groaned as she stirred from bed.

"Rest, lass," a voice with a thick accent said.

"Adair?"

She felt her wings and noticed one was completely bandaged. "I stitched your wing. It should be good as new after a while."

Anger welled up inside her. She tore at the bandages. "No. I want them gone."

"Leave 'em alone, Raven. They need to heal."

"I want them gone!" she yelled, lashing out at him. "Remove them from me. I don't want them."

The dwarf seized her hands. "Thrion! Git in here. I need yer help!"

"Take them from me! Rid me of these wings!" She moved her wing as adrenaline shot through her limbs.

Thrion rushed in. "Enough!" he roared.

He wrapped his arm around her. She froze, crying into his chest. "Adair is going to look at your wing now. Is that all right?"

She jerked her head, meeting his gaze. "Only if he cuts them. They've brought me nothing but pain."

"They are a gift from Asteral. They aren't ours to give or take."

She gave a bitter laugh. "You talk as if you know the burden of keeping a part of yourself hidden. You know nothing!" she yelled. "Nothing!"

Thrion rose, turning his back to her. Without a word, he removed his tunic.

Selest gasped. Twin scars protruded from his back. Winged scars. "I d-don't—H-how—"

He knelt beside her. "I pray you'll refrain from making such rash remarks after you hear my tale of how I lost them." He sighed. "My mother was the Virtue of Spring who came to marry her apprentice, my father. We resided in the Misty Forest in a quaint cottage.

"Every autumn my father invited a few archangelic foresters into his home when they would come to hunt game under the order of the Baron of Fallendell. I was a young lad and had seen ten winters. Every year I wanted to join the merry men in their wild hunt. That year my father was away at the time of the hunt. But before he left, and after much convincing, I won o'er his permission and joined the young men upon the chase of a wild stag for the Midwinter Feast.

"We were clad in green cloaks and adorned with buckskins with our arrows nocked and aimed to kill our prize. Alas, my arrogance got the best of me and I was the first to fire. I missed, and the stag alighted.

"We were afoot, so the chase proved difficult. We split up in hopes of cornering the beast. Some took to the treetops above, whilst I was on the ground. After much struggle, we finally tracked it down nigh to Dwindloth's stony ridge. Now that it was cornered, we took our aim and killed the beast for good."

His gaze saddened. "Or so we thought. Alas, we were oblivious to the devilry that ensued. For the stag was truly a hag under a cloaking spell, and she led us to our tomb."

Silence enveloped the room. "I fled to the safety of the mountains and hid in a stony cavern. Alas, I could hear the foresters' cries from whence I hid. Their bloodcurdling entreaties rang in my ears as the crones removed their wings—all before ending the foresters' lives with their daggers. My cries were intermingled with theirs, yet mine were drowned out by the sounds of slaughter.

"I know not how long I remained in the shadows of that cave. Darkness had fallen o'er the gloom of that funerary night. I waited and begged Asteral for silence to prevail. But it didn't. The heathens' celebratory cries joined their victims' damned pleas for help.

"It drove me mad to the point where I couldn't bear it any longer. So I made the daring attempt to flee. I stumbled from my hiding place, and ascended into the sky, praying the cover of night would be enough to escape.

"Yet as I flew o'er the massacre, I beheld a sight straight from Hell. The heathens were performing their rites and feasting on their victims' flesh. Once they finished consuming their flesh, they adorned themselves with their skulls and bones. And their wings." He choked. "Their wings were laid upon the ground, neatly cut and laid out upon symbols of blood. I was terrified thus, and could not contain my scream of horror.

"The witches saw me in the sky and shrieked murderous curses too cruel to utter. They pursued me from below as I flew homeward. The journey proved difficult as my poor wings were weighed down by the long journey. But I pressed onward, praying I would return alive to the comfort of my mother's arms."

Fear grew in his gray eyes. "But my poor wings grew limp with weariness and I had no choice but to land amongst the treetops. I prayed I'd be safe until dawn.

"It was hours of endless silence before they found me. They cackled maniacally as they climbed the trees. They pulled me down to the ground and forced me onto my belly as they whetted their sacrificial knife."

Tears welled in his eyes. "Bit by bit, they cut away my wings. The pain was beyond words and I can still feel the cold blade piercing through my skin to this day."

Tears streamed down Selest's eyes, her own wounds still throbbing. "H-how did you escape?"

Thrion sniffed and dabbled his tears with his hand. "By the guidance of Asteral, I was just close enough to home when a man heard my desperate pleas. He stood against my foe, wielding a torch of flame. He startled the heathens long enough to aid me in my plight.

"He grabbed me in his arms and ran as fast as he could for the cottage. He warned my mother, who had just returned from searching for me since we were supposed to have returned by nightfall.

"She called upon the wrath of the heavens and sent down torrents of wind to subdue the pursuing evil. After she had killed them, she tended to my wounds, and we anxiously awaited my father's return..."

"...and your father helped mine in exchange," concluded Selest.

Thrion nodded. "So you say I don't know your pain? I wake up every day mourning the loss of my wings. They were a gift from Asteral. But you say you want them taken from you when they're not yours to take?"

"I'd rather my wings be taken now before they're taken by someone cruel and vile like the Shaden merchants o-or witches," she sobbed.

Thrion knelt beside her. "I won't allow you to endure the same fate I had to endure."

Adair peered at her reassuringly. "Aye. None o' us will."

Selest eyed her trembling hand. "Can you save me from myself?"

Thrion placed a hand on her shoulder. "Father above, may Selest find peace in your embrace. Amen."

"Amen," mumbled Adair. After he tended to her torn wing, he urged her to go to bed early.

So that night Selest rested in the comfort of her bed. Nightmares of Thrion's story haunted her dreams.

Each day that passed, her wounds healed, but the nightmares festered. Each day that passed was one day closer to the Council.

Chapter 19

"Again!" Selest swung her staff at a wooden post in the training arena. Faern instructed her.

"Relax your grip, and spread your hands apart a bit. If you were to counter the Temptress right now, what would you do?"

Morbid images flashed through her mind. Her grip grew slick with sweat.

"I'd observe her weaker points."

"Counterattacks are good." Faern nodded. "And then what advantage would you take?"

"I could—create a diversion, I suppose."

"And?"

"And I could leap back, using my wings to send me airborne."

"You're describing the same tactic you used on Adair," Faern said. "Never use the same move twice in the enemy's eyes, or else you'll lose your element of surprise."

Faern raised his weapon. "Be sure to keep your swings fluid and efficient."

Warily she advanced, but just out of the centaur's reach. The centaur swung his sword. It sliced the air with deadly precision.

Thoughts welled up inside her mind. Her father. The Glade. The entire West.

She shook in rage. The cries. The enemy. Zyon's losses. The pain. Her wings. The evil doings of this world.

The Key pulsed against her side as she swung her staff at him.

Sweat dripped from her brow until she finally stumbled to the ground. Faern had her at swordpoint.

Selest panted heavily.

Faern offered her a hand. "You must control your blows, and use your weapon with a purpose, instead of swinging it blindly about."

Panting, she nodded.

"Don't let your emotions govern you in a fight or it'll be your downfall. If you're aware of these mistakes and strive to fix them, you'll be better off."

She sighed. "Yessir."

Faern nodded.

"Faern—"

"Hm?"

"Do you really think I have what it takes?"

"You have the spirit of a fighter. After all, you did throw yourself between Thrion and that Shadower. That is the quality of a true warrior. I think we can make something of you yet."

Her mouth formed a meek smile. "Thank you."

"Now, shall we go again?" he said, gripping his lance.

Nodding, she picked up her staff once more, relaxing her grip.

"Swing again," Faern instructed.

Selest hit the wooden pole over and over.

"Faster."

Selest tuned into the tempo of the blows. One-two, one-two. But now at a quicker pace. One-two-three-four, one-two-three-four. Her focus blurred into the beat of a song. A song from Starry Eve years ago.

> *The same cold breeze*
> *That rustles the leaves*
> *Blows forth an icy gale*
> *Spiraling a misty veil*
> *Creating spirits soaring free*
> *The same cold breeze...*

"You are good at finding your rhythm," Faern commented. "And by doing just that, you'll find newer rhythms—less constant and more chaotic as it will be in battle." She was thrilled at that perspective.

Suddenly, a cluster of shadows swirled overhead.

Her gaze drifted upwards to a group of winged steeds. They circled the perimeter and landed in the middle of the courtyard.

She stared in awe, for she couldn't recall the last time she laid eyes upon a steed as valiant and as noble as the pegasus. The winged horses bore coats as white as pearls, with magnificent wings to carry them across the untamed Skyland.

In the sunlight, they gleamed as orange and white stars in the day. The pegasuses were angel's mounts for transportation whether it be to deliver news or fight in a war.

Her eyes widened. It was the angels of S'iara and Glascia.

As she got a better view of the pegasuses and their riders, she noted their matching bronze armor gleaming in the sunlight. Their deep orange garments rippled in the wind.

Just then the thunder of hooves announced the arrival of more attendees at the entrance gate. The steeds were of many shades of silver and white. Their tails flamed with iridescent light casting an unearthly aura about them.

At the forefront rode an angel of grander status. He was clad in the purest of golden armor and armed with a longsword that glinted in the sunlight.

It was Alessenger, son of Father Harvest.

The angel's features were grim and lined with many creases of battle-worn vengeance. His hair gleamed a weathered red around a dark face, his golden eyes grim.

But what was most remarkable was the single brown wing he bore.

The brown was touched with a hue of gold, much like his sister's.

Selest recalled reading that his other wing was lost in the wretched Shadow War, hewn by the Nephilim of Zithera. But in spite of his loss, he rode with a gallant grandeur, wearing his battle scars with pride. It was so with the entire company of S'iara.

"Hail, my brothers." His voice rang as pure as a golden trumpet.

Dismounting, he started forth to greet his sister.

Orla rushed to her brother. "Alessenger! I expected you to return three days before the day of the Council. Why are you here prematurely?"

Her brother placed a hand on her shoulder, his eyes grave. "Come. There's much to discuss."

Selest and the company gathered in the banquet hall.

"What's happening?" Selest asked Faern. "Why have they arrived so early?"

"Something is amiss," replied the centaur.

As they seated themselves, Alessenger stood before them. "Glascian spies have spotted demons traveling on the edge of their borders. Nephilim were also spotted flying above S'iara."

"They didn't attack?" asked Adhearn.

"No. They are likely planning something," Alessenger paused. "I've reason to believe they plan to attack the day of the Council."

Murmurs crescendoed in the halls.

Yaelas stepped forth. "The witches' reclaiming of the West was just the beginning. I deem that the evil which lurks will stop at nothing to repossess the entire Inner Realm."

"You're right," said Alessenger, peering at the company. "Already too many lives have been spent."

"Then we must call the Council off," Orla declared.

"Wait," said Selest. "There's something else you should know."

Alessenger's eyes stared into her very core. "What is it?" Silence. "Speak!" he commanded.

With a trembling hand, she withdrew the Key from her pocket.

Everyone gasped. "It can't be. How is this yours to bear?" he whispered in awe.

"'Twas my father's. After the witches attacked my home, he gave it to me and said to fulfill the Quest of the Key."

Alessenger clamped his jaw shut, considering her words as their eyes locked. "Then the time has come for the Quest to be fulfilled."

The color drained from Selest's face. The Key slipped from her hand. "M-me—?" She shook her head. "I'm sorry but—"

"You can't escape the will of Asteral, child," replied Alessenger.

She picked up the Key and examined it in her hand, the crystal taunting her in the candlelight.

She peered at her companions. They rose from their seats, smiling at her reassuringly. She sighed. They were loyal to each other. And yet, perhaps too loyal.

Thrion approached her. "We are with you."

She smiled.

Alessenger cleared his throat. "We'll let them come, and we'll be ready. The war shall be a diversion. Then you will fulfill the Quest and rid us of this evil."

Alessenger addressed Selest. "Might I suggest you take a guide? Perhaps Yaelas?"

The warlock stepped forth joining Selest, Thrion, Faern, and Adair.

Alessenger turned to Orla. "Send your swiftest messengers throughout the realm. Tell them to prepare for battle."

Nodding, she dashed out of the room.

Alessenger looked at each of them. "By the day they attack we'll be one step ahead. This war shall be a diversion. We'll hold the enemy at bay as best we can, while you fulfill the Quest of the Key."

"Many years ago," Yaelas added, "the Quest failed, and my wife perished. Yet no matter the cost, we're all united by the will of Asteral. We shall see it through."

Selest gave a thin smile and turned to leave the banquet hall. "I think I'm going to retire for the remainder of the evening." She quietly added, "Though I wouldn't mind some company."

Thrion rose from his seat. "I'd be happy to accompany you, lass."

Her face reddened. "T-thank you, Thrion."

As they strolled leisurely through the courtyard, the blue glow of evening cascading over the walls, Selest halted by the fountain.

"How are you?" Thrion turned to face her, his gray eyes mirroring the lonely twilight.

She sighed. "I've been better." She stole a glance at him. "But I suppose this fine evening makes up for it." She wrung her skirts. "Thrion?"

"Yes? What is it, lass?"

"H-how are things with you and your father?"

Silence.

"I-I'm sorry I asked."

"Your concern is very much appreciated. Yet, I don't know the words to answer that question."

Selest's heart poured out to him. Yaelas had kept the Quest and the Key a secret from him, as her father had from her. She understood that level of betrayal.

"If there's anything I can do to help you, let me know."

Selest gave him a tight smile. "Thank you, Thrion."

Thrion nodded. "After his revelation, my father and I took a stroll in the courtyard, and we discussed all that has befallen us, as well as the Key. It was hard, I admit, but it was progress."

"Are you afraid?" she whispered. "What if our attempt to fulfill the Quest fails like our parents' attempt?"

"I rest my fears in this knowledge: the Key is to fulfill Asteral's purpose and to be rid of the evil that dominates His realm, and then the Inner Realm will be free, and beyond."

Selest pondered his words. "It's getting late. I think I should get some rest for the journey ahead."

Thrion turned to leave. "Yes. Well, good night. I'll see you in the morning."

As she entered her room, her stomach was full of dread. Silently, she shut the door and dressed in her nightgown.

She didn't sleep that night.

Instead, she lay there thinking of what was yet to come. She grasped the Key.

The thought of what lay beyond Hell's door haunted her like a living nightmare.

Selest peered at the ceiling, searching, wondering for an answer hidden just beyond her knowledge. "Asteral, what am I to do? If it is Your will, why didn't others before me succeed? How will I know I won't endure the same fate?" She squeezed her eyes shut as she prayed.

As the night slowly ticked by amid preparations for the journey, the wizard spent his time mapping their course. He decided they'd march northwest across Orai, making for Forbid.

The next morning, they made ready to depart. As the company prepared to mount their steeds, Alessenger and Orla said a prayer over them. "Asteral may You watch over these five brave souls as they venture forth today," began Alessenger. "May the Key of Raining Glass fulfill Asteral's prophecy. In your name, amen."

They exchanged final goodbyes. Selest looked ahead at the endless plains that stretched out before them, clenching at the Key in her cloak pocket.

Thrion, Yaelas, and Adair spoke with Alessenger as Faern said his goodbyes to Astria.

"So I guess this is farewell then." Oskari approached, his brown eyes full of sadness.

Selest gave him a sad smile. "We don't know that."

"Heh." The faun wiped away his tears. "I owe ya one Selest. Ya saved my sorry hide."

Selest smiled. "What are friends for?"

Oskari blinked back tears. "I would go with ya, but a musician like me isn't of much need on a Quest such as yers."

Selest placed a hand on his shoulder. "Until we meet again, be it in this life or in the Eternal Sky."

Oskari returned the gesture. "We fauns in Brandemere will write songs about ya, Selest, mark my words."

"All right, everyone, move out!" cried Yaelas. As Selest mounted her horse, she turned in her saddle. "Oh, Oskari? When you get to writing that song of yours, make sure to draw from the Song of Elarael. It's one of my favorite poems."

A smile spread across the faun's face. "Will do." He waved.

Selest waved back before joining the others.

They were given three steeds. Selest's steed was a white pinto from the plains of S'iara. She drew up beside Thrion who was astride a blue roan. Adair was seated behind Thrion.

Yaelas rode ahead astride a dappled gray gelding, conversing with Faern regarding the journey ahead.

She turned to look into Thrion's eyes, which were hardened and resolute to face whatever horror was to come.

It was unbearable to leave the gleaming house of Orai as they traveled north to the edge of Forbid. Their former place of refuge glistened like a star in the golden fields of Heaven. Seeing it from a distance was like floating on the edge of a miraged dream in the misty morning in the bleak Ashlands.

Selest glanced behind her longingly as the fortitude of hope vanished altogether amid the silvery fog.

She trotted alongside Thrion and Adair. Selest fidgeted with her reins. "So Thrion, I'm just curious—what type of wings did you have? What were they like? Were you an owl-wing like me, a crow-wing of Falendell, or a falcon-wing of Orai? Do you still consider yourself an archangel?"

Thrion was quiet. The air grew tense. Adair's brows rose at Selest's badgering.

"I-I'm sorry Thrion, I meant no offense. Curiosity's gotten the better of me."

Thrion sighed. "No, no, it's all right. To answer your question, yes, I still consider myself one. I had wings like yours, but mine were pure white in color, with the slightest of silver dew. 'Twas in the likeness of my mother—" The mere utterance of his words proved laborious.

Selest peered at the horizon. "You know what I think, Thrion?"

"What?"

"Your scars tell of a tragic story. Yet I think it was only the beginning. Maybe in the end you'll get wings grander than ever before."

Thrion smiled. "Perhaps."

The journey pressed the weary travelers on as time frayed away. The days passed by under darkened rain clouds filled with booming thunder. The stretch of golden fields turned to a muddled brown.

Yaelas said they were on the edge of the Orain border. It smelled of damp rain, as well as manure from the nearby pastures of grazing sheep.

After moments of intense silence, they continued on until the river Etchemere came into view. The silver courses of water ran through Orai providing fish for their supper.

Suddenly, a piercing shriek rang in Selest's ears and sent her blood running cold.

"Everyone, this way, quickly." Yaelas led them to an outcropping of gray rocks where they waited.

Amid her toil along the rough terrain, she dared a glance at the blinding steel-colored horizon.

Against it, shapes stood out in contrast to the dreary sky. Her heart turned to stone. Nephilim. She recalled reading of such creatures. They were winged demons who resided in the wastelands of Zithera.

They were like bats, swooping down and seizing sheep with their bare hands.

The deafening shrieks of the ewes pierced the air as they were snatched away.

The Nephilim soon spotted the travelers and swooped down to attack. Selest gasped, staring in shock into the abysmal eyes of the enemy.

Faern overtook the Nephilim within his reach. The mighty centaur reared, slashing his sword. Thrion pierced what enemy he could with his arrows. Suddenly, one threatened to overwhelm him.

Thrion rushed into the open, nocking an arrow. He aimed at the

Nephilim and pierced its skull.

Selest's eyes widened. "Watch out!"

A black shadow seized Thrion. Selest dashed into the fray.

"Raven!"

Raising her staff, she drove it into the Nephilim's neck. A shriek escaped from its lips, making Selest's blood run cold.

A hand struck her.

Stunned, she fell to the ground but quickly spread and flexed her wings, rising above the battle and straining not to fall.

The Nephilim advanced, raising its spear. Trembling, her wings gave out, and she crashed into the mud. Her heart raced with adrenaline.

Selest prayed to Asteral above. Suddenly, a volley of arrows rained down. A blur of gray clouded her vision. A staff pierced through the Nephilim. It fell dead at her feet.

Thrion seized her out of the fray and they watched as the Nephilim retreated from whence they came.

"Nephilim scouts are taking control of the neighboring village. The time they seek to strike is nigh," said the wizard. "Hurry! We must be on our way. They will send reinforcements."

They continued on for some time finally settling under an overhanging rock for the night.

Selest slept deeply, waking to a crackling fire and a pounding headache. Her vision blurred in and out of focus. She could discern it was dark. Whether it was the heavy clouds above or the time of day, she did not know. Absent-mindedly, she squinted in the dim light.

She groaned with fatigue as she propped herself into a sitting position against a nearby rock. Peering warily about her, she spied Faern and Adair by the fire.

She heard muffled voices as the party conversed. She could smell the rain mixed with smoke. Then she remembered the massacre.

Thrion returned with a deer hanging limp on his shoulder. He unsheathed a knife and began skinning it, cutting off the fat and selecting the best meats to roast.

"How's the fire coming?" Thrion called over his shoulder.

"The fire will be roaring in no time," said Adair.

"What of the smell? It could attract unwanted guests." Thrion glanced to and fro in anxious wariness.

"Don't worry, I sprinkled an herb to mask the smell," Adair reassured everyone. "We are well hidden under the cloak of night."

He made a makeshift turner with sticks and large rocks, and placed the deer on the spit, turning it above the fire.

Selest's mouth watered at the delicious sight and smell, in spite of the dreary forecast above them and the looming forest ahead.

He raised the deer on the stick and set it on a makeshift platter made from bark. They ate in silence below the waning crescent. As they ate their fill, Thrion had the others set to work preserving fresh-cut meats for the road ahead.

"What are your plans if the Quest succeeds?" Their attention turned to her. She glanced at each of them in turn. "What do you plan to do with your lives?"

Faern shifted uneasily. "I do not think of such fancies. I only take things one at a time. But considering the 'if'—I deem I would return to the Emerald Dells and see them restored to the same green of many eras ago."

Adair stared at the flames, thinking. "I plan to reclaim the Silver Mountains. He looked longingly westward. "I wish to set my eyes on those glorious caverns that gleam with chandeliers of pure gem light. I wish to hear that merry hum of mining in rhythm to the falling of the dwarven hammers."

In her mind's eye, Selest saw the pictures as clear and bright as if they were in Crysil's Mirror.

"What of you, lass?" asked Adair.

Selest peered into his eyes, as blue as a snowy sky. "I want to write books and tell stories of adventures."

Faern folded his arms. "Well, you shall have a tale or two of your own to tell."

She smiled. "I hope to return to The Glade and write those stories." Her smile faded. "Alas, it seems only a dream."

Adair fiddled with a piece of bark. "But it could turn into a reality, Raven. Ye ne'er know."

Later that night, Selest took the first watch. She sat on a gray boulder near the fire and watched intently.

As she scanned the forest, a great figure cloaked in night shadow and tree shade seemed to approach. Her blood ran cold. She had a white-knuckled grip on her staff. *It's just the shadows playing tricks on me.* A ghostly cry pierced the night like a forgotten eulogy. A chill ran down her spine.

She glanced at the large maw lined with fork-like trees.

"Wake up." She turned to her sleeping companions. "I saw something peculiar in the trees."

They stirred.

A lamenting sound carried throughout the forest and pierced the heavens.

The echoes were lingering shadows. Unseen. Heard by lost souls. Rain fell.

The cry was carried out along the single path they trod.

"This forest is full of trickery," said Adair. "Selest, git some rest. Let us take the second watch."

She reluctantly did so. But as she slept, those same eyes haunted her. They were searching, hunting for something that was in her possession. She clutched her pocket. She felt like a cornered animal, trapped, with nowhere to go.

Chapter 20

Selest woke miserably to a cold predawn. The forest shadow ensnared them all. The company breakfasted on berries and mushrooms sitting upon the damp leaves.

"We are here," Yaelas pointed at the upper center of the map. "We must travel westward to reach the Silver Mountains."

"By Darragh," exclaimed Adair, "ne'er have I dreamed of entering into the mountain halls of my forefathers."

Selest's eyes widened as she studied the map. "Wait—we have to travel through the witches' forest?"

Faern shifted uncomfortably. "It's the quickest route to the mountains. But keep in mind, the further we travel, the more we must vary our route. Even if we dare trace the mere borderline we must be careful. Even our cloaks of camouflage will prove inadequate against the witches' spells."

Thrion rose. "Our cloaks will do fine as long as we cover our tracks and mask our scent." He turned to Adair. "You do not happen to have any Veiler's Thyme on you?"

Adair looked at Thrion as though he was crazy. "Travel southwest of here to the Graven Coast if you want your precious herb. Veiler's Thyme is a tropical herb. It doesn't grow in these parts."

"But doesn't Gorm Buaic trade with Cair Gaoth?"

"Aye, for warring purposes. But last time I checked we were at peace until—four months ago."

"Is there another way to mask our scent then?" asked Selest.

Thrion stared at the fire. "If we soak our cloaks in the deer's entrails."

Selest felt sick to her stomach.

Yaelas considered this. "I pray the witches do not pick up our scent. Defiling our cloaks must suffice."

"We should scout the forest beyond," said the hunter.

"Thrion and I shall go on ahead and find a trail for safe passage," Yaelas announced.

Selest's heart dropped to her feet. "Be careful," she said, her brows furrowed.

Thrion's mouth formed a tight smile.

Selest caught a glance of Thrion looking back before disappearing into the dark boughs of Forbid.

After breakfast, they got to work on the revolting task that involved their cloaks and then gathered their provisions.

Later that day, Thrion and his father emerged from the forest.

"We've found an abandoned monastery we can take shelter in," said Thrion.

As silent as the forest's solitude, the company rode into Forbid.

Being at the edge of the forest was as suffocating as it was inside. The very air was harder to breathe as they ventured farther and farther into the depths. Dimmer and dimmer it got, until the eerie spell of the trees blocked out the sun entirely. The forest felt like a cold, still morn frozen in a time of gravestone lands and unseen horrors. A crow, as black as death, cawed upon a branch overhead. The trees stood like the reaper's minions, staring at them with unseen shadow eyes. And still on they went. As far as the company could see, thin mist enshrouded their surroundings, making things appear remote and otherworldly.

Time passed like a waterwheel grinding the grains of their minds until a drought was all that was left. And still on they went; one foot in front of the next, ever on into oblivion. Soon, that phantom waterwheel became a reality. There it was—an old house that bore the device meant for grinding grain, unturning and abandoned. There the procession stopped. The company was grateful for the rest, though once they halted an eerie presence overtook Selest. She shifted uneasily as she peered into the forest.

The company turned its attention to the old building. A thin wail sounded in the wind. Words formed so tangible and so ghostly they were loath to breathe the very air those words penetrated.

A haunting eulogy blew in the wind. Selest's discerned these words:

> We wander these lands
> Cast from Asteral's right hand
> Ne'er to see brighter days
> Our quest is unending fore'er and always
> This eulogy is our cry: We are broken
> Our hearts have awoken
> To the realm of false reality
> For all isn't as it seemed
> Unto us and unto creed
> We are the seed
> Left unplanted and unreaped
> We've been planted into deep
> Unattended to by the farmer's scythe
> In the pain of abandonment, we writhe
> Reborn from the graveyard's womb

Lamenting nigh the witch's tomb
We march as the scrapers' throng
Fulfilling our desire so we can belong
To regain what was lost
No matter the cost
We daren't tarry
Bones we must bury
None are nigh to heed their death
Until the world's last dying breath

All at once, the eulogy ceased and the eerie silence enveloped them once more.

"What was that?" whispered Selest.

"Witchcraft," Thrion replied. "Stay close. The farther in we venture, the more we'll be lured away from our course." Just like what happened at the Fields of Shile.

Selest shivered. Yaelas beckoned them to follow. "Come, let us leave this foul place. Remember, stick close." Selest heeded his words as they traveled onward, the cold eyes of the house with the mill gaping after them.

Whatever days that passed were all but unknown to them. It was ever so cold and grim that the sun became but a memory. They hungered for the taste of food and thirsted for the freshness of the water, cold and clear. Fatigue trailed their footsteps until it crawled on their skin, and possessed them with dimmed minds. But still, they marched on unfazed and unheeding.

After walking listlessly and silently northward, they came upon the stark silhouette of a building. As they got closer, with weary eyes they discerned an old monastery. The stone building was dark and dreary, reeking of age and decay.

Gray ivy covered the stone. Selest thought it was as though the dreary building was hiding behind a facade of a holy fortress in hopes of trying to hide a dark secret.

A wailing lament accompanied the morbid scene.

They drew their weapons, warily circling the building, searching for the horrid source.

"Here!" shouted Yaelas. He tore at strands of ivy and revealed a side door.

Faern brought down the rotted door with a swift stroke of a sword.

Yaelas was the first to enter, summoning light from his staff and illuminating the room in a soft blue glow.

As they entered, Selest wrinkled her nose. It smelled of rat droppings and rot. Manuscripts littered the floor. Tables and chairs lay scattered and splintered.

"This must've been an ambush." Thrion scanned the perimeter.

"Aye. Fairly recent too," agreed Adair, tracing blood-stained cobblestone with a gloved finger.

Selest had a white-knuckled grip on her staff. The wailing reverberated beneath her feet. She jumped in surprise. "It sounds like it's coming from below. They must be held hostage somewhere down there."

Thrion tapped on the floor, tracing the cracks in the stone. "There should be an entrance nigh."

Yaelas tapped on the walls with his staff. Selest did the same.

After a few moments, Yaelas struck a hollow point in the wall. "Here!" The wizard withdrew a tapestry, revealing a barred door.

Selest approached. "Is there a keyhole intact?"

The wizard shook his head. "I fear not. We will have to use force."

"Here." Faern uncovered a piece of timber amid the wreckage. "Thrion, Adair, help me bring down the door."

The three grabbed hold of the piece of wood, poised to smash the door with full momentum.

"Now!" They rushed forward, ramming the timber against the heavily bolted door. After a few swings, it finally gave away and split in two.

Selest timidly approached the empty maw.

Beyond the debris, she discovered a stairwell leading down into a dark chasm.

"I'm going down there. Who's coming with me?" Yaelas peered at each one in turn as he stepped forward. Thrion clapped Adair and Selest on the shoulders. "The three of us ought to go as well."

"I'll keep watch," said Faern. The centaur fingered the hilt of his lance. "The rest of you, be careful down there."

"I-I think I'll stay behind as well," Adair said with a quiet voice.

Selest raised her brows. "And I thought I was the only scared one," she said, wringing her hands upon her staff.

"No, Raven, you are not."

"I'm scared Adair—petrified even. But there's someone down there who needs our help, and I'd rather not wait around as he continues to suffer."

"I—" Adair hesitated. "I-if you're going down there, then I best go too. He quickly added, "Wouldn't want anything happening to ya anyway. Zyon did entrust me to care for ya after all."

Selest smiled.

"It is settled then," said Yaelas. "Let's go."

Yaelas summoned the full extent of his lighted staff to combat the darkness. "Come, this way." He led them down the twisting stairs to the bottom where a row of prison cells stretched beyond the light. The wailing was more present than ever, and so real it sounded like the tortured cries of Hell.

The air about them was damp and smelled of decay.

The scene seemed to be the very embodiment of the moans and groans of the tormented soul ahead.

As they continued to follow the sound, the air grew heavy as the walls seemed to close in around them.

Selest's entire body was damp with a foul reek. She squinted amid the darkness, scoping out the perimeter.

She shivered. The cries were so wretched that Selest wanted to rip her ears off. The cries around her were the definition of treachery.

After winding through a long narrow hallway they entered a gap in the wall.

There the dim light was replaced by pitch blackness with only the hint of light at the end. It was like walking in a tunnel and straining to reach the end. The more progress they made, they were sure they saw a light. Not a warm bright yellow light, but a firelight that had never known the brightness of day.

The sound of their footsteps crescendoed into an eerie lament as they entered a large chamber lit by the haunting fire.

Selest's heart grew cold. She clutched her staff defensively, for this was death's bloody womb.

There in the center lay a sight that would rest forever in her bosom. Skulls littered the floor, and blood was painted on the walls in Xithe, the old tongue of dark chants.

Pairs of wings littered the stone floor.

Selest turned away.

Yaelas urged them onward. "Come, let's keep moving." They exited the room, proceeding through the hallway until it abruptly came to an end. Before them lay a door.

Thrion tried to open it, but as soon as he laid a hand upon the latch a shock jolted him.

"A dark spell is upon this door. I cannot open it."

"The Key," Yaelas said. "The Key of Ezelex shall set the captives free." The wizard turned to the company. "Selestial Inriser, Bearer of the Key, I bid you come forth and set the captives free." His voice boomed. "These tortured souls are in imperative danger, and only you have possession of that power to release them."

Select strode forth in shock. It happened so suddenly that she dared not hesitate. She rushed to where he was.

"Hail, the company of a New Day, come and help her bear it. Listen to me, all of you," Yaelas demanded. "We are about to enter within in hopes to save these captive souls. We, as the company of Asteral's Key, have been called."

Thrion placed a hand on Yaelas' shoulder. "Father, are you certain of this?"

Select stepped forward. "No, Thrion, he's right."

"Select, one of us can do it, you don't have to—"

The wailing was now a close shriek piercing the air.

"End me! Woe pain, woe suffering! Let it cease!"

She trembled as she withdrew the Key from her pocket. "It was entrusted to me by my father, and I will not turn back now if any are in danger."

Thrion gave a firm nod. "Do what you must."

She approached the door in the shadow and, spotting the keyhole, slid in the Key and unlocked it. The door burst open to a single hallway dimly lit by ruby-red torches. A coldness none of them had felt before seeped through their bones, freezing them beyond numbness. Yaelas entered the singular fortress first, followed by the rest. Before them, another door stood with two eyes peering out darkly through a meager opening.

She took a deep breath and advanced forward past Yaelas, bracing herself against the possessor's icy-hot stare. When she came to the door, the shadow weighed her heart with such suffocating stiffness that she nearly doubled over. Regardless, she steadied herself as she forced the Key into the keyhole and opened the door.

A figure collapsed from its prison. She barely discerned the face but noticed it was a man. His features were so frail and thin, she thought a ghost was before her.

He fell down on his face at Selest's feet. A haunted voice spoke: "O archangel of light, hast thou come to leadeth me to Heaven's door?"

Her eyes widened.

"My body is dust in the bitterest of glooms," he continued, lifting his head. "I am broken beyond repair." His voice was detached, as though speaking only to the darkness itself. He shivered uncontrollably, his eyes darting this way and that.

Select tried to soothe the bereaved man. "It's all right, you're amongst friends."

The monk suddenly began clawing at her as if just noticing he was not alone. "Ye must get out! This place will be your tomb!"

Thrion rushed between the two. Immediately, Adair hastened to the monk's side, withdrawing calming herbs from his satchel in hopes to ease the man's unsettled state.

He lashed out once more. Thrion and Yaelas restrained him as Adair held the herb to his nose. Instantly the flailing man calmed. "Deep breaths, lad. Deep breaths. Steady now, he does it."

The monk calmed. "We—" he rasped, "We have to get out."

"Ya don't have to tell me twice," Adair muttered.

Selest caressed his hand. "Shhh. You're safe now. Everything will soon be well."

His eyelids fluttered shut and his hand relaxed.

Thrion hoisted the man's frail body over his shoulder. "Come, let's leave this foul place. There are no other living souls here."

The monk swung back and forth, as limp as a sack of grain. The motion reminded Selest of the pendulum of death, slowly ticking down their moments below ground as they continued on. Selest shivered, her entire body screaming to escape the tomb.

No wonder the poor man went mad down here. He was all alone surrounded by his brethren killed by the Shadowers.

As they continued down the hall of the prison, Selest noticed bloody symbols like the ones Thrion described in his horrid account of the Nephilim.

She shivered, dread weighing upon her chest.

The monk gave a bitter laugh. "I deem *they* will be present—no one goeth in or out without *their* consent."

Adair stopped short. "Who is 'they'?"

The monk lowered his voice to a whisper as though evil spirits might be eavesdropping. "*They* weareth cloaks wrought of darkness, and their eyes art as red as hellfire. They have faces of the abyss."

"The Eleven?" whispered Selest. "Shadowers?"

The man's eyes widened with terror. "Ye've seen them too?"

"Yes," Selest rasped, trembling as images of the blade flashed through her mind. The screams in her mind seemed to echo through the dark chambers.

Yaelas' staff grew with light. "This way."

The monk mumbled a verse, "Yea, though I walk through the valley of the shadow of death, I will fear no evil: for thou art with me; Thy rod and thy staff they comfort me."

The verse eased her soul. How enlightening those words were in such dark times. The verse echoed through the chambers of the abyss, through the dungeons, and through the occultist's dwelling—even through her very being.

It planted a seed of hope in all their hearts.

Suddenly, Selest noticed a gaping hole in the wall.

Her heart pounded. "We're close!"

The faint outline of the stairwell came into view.

"This way!" Yaelas cried. "Ladies first. Watch your step."

Selest raced up the steps and burst into the room, slamming into the centaur's chest. She got the wind knocked out of her as she tried to catch her breath.

Faern steadied her. "Thank Celtan's Bow you made it out. I was beginning to worry."

Selest shook uncontrollably. "It was awful, Faern. Truly awful." The centaur held her in an embrace, stroking her hair. "Shhh. You're safe now."

As Thrion approached, Faern noticed the limp form of the captive. "Ah, I see you've found the source of lament."

"Yes. I fear he's the last survivor." Thrion explained their recent discovery.

The centaur furrowed his brow, stroking Selest's wings. "Why does such cruelty exist amongst heavenly beings?"

Faern aided the monk from the stairs.

The monk withdrew his hood revealing a thin, pale face. His mousey brown hair ringed his head like a halo about his bald scalp. His dark green eyes flickered with urgency.

The monk peered at the destroyed monastery.

Selest's heart went out to him. For many months he had been held captive there. And now he was free from his prison, yet the stirring of evil remained in the very depth of his heart. Only he had survived out of all that had been there.

"I knoweth these walls," he said. "Yet now they're full of rot and decay. Our captors art not too far away. Already many of my brothers hath been slain. I do not desire the same fate to befall thee."

The monk wandered about and they followed him into the main hall.

"Were you—an archangel?" Thrion asked, perplexed.

He nodded, paralyzed with fear. "When Asteral stripped the Eleven of their wings, they did whatever was in their evil power to get them back, even if it meant roaming the Inner Realm." He cleared his throat and continued. "They cameth in the night and captured my brethren and me. My brothers and I were here for countless months. We tried to escape. We searched every nook and cranny, only to lose ourselves to the darkness. Now the cries of my brothers shepherd the way to lost souls. But even the thought is hopeless. Everything meets darkness and darkness meets no end. I've feasted on sluggish things that inhabit here. And we drink the very dampness the sowers provide. W-we were stripped of our wings, and the cruel devils spoketh evil spells o'er our heavenly vessels within a ritual to regain their own."

He rocked back and forth on his heels. "They would not cease. Nay. They killed every one of my brethren in their evil vices."

"What kind of archangels were you?" asked Selest, taking his hand in an attempt to soothe him.

"Falendell."

Selest's heart raced. "How long were you down there?"

"Let the poor man rest, lass. Save yer questions," the dwarf responded in a firm but gentle tone as he prepared to examine the monk's wounds.

The monk placed a frail hand on the dwarf's arm. "Nay, nay, 'tis fine."

He turned to Selest. "Forty days I heard the screams of my brethren." Tears welled in his eyes. "Forty hellish days I endured, again and again, wondering if I was next," he sobbed.

Selest squeezed his hand.

After a while, the monk regained his composure. "T-they made this holy place their temple. They were of Asteral's triad once, but He took their wings after they swore allegiance to the Deceptor. Their wings were everything to them; they did whatever it took to reclaim what they had lost." The monk shivered. "They traveleth far and wide under the guise of cloak and dark magick to search out whatever is needed to fulfill their desire for restoration."

"We first encountered them on the Fields of Shile, and they chased us to Snowtown," said Thrion. "They've been after us ever since."

For a moment, his green eyes flickered with hope. "Snowtown? P-pray tell, was one of my fellow brethren amongst them?"

Thrion nodded, withdrawing a necklace and fingering the star. "You guessed right, Brother."

"Praise to Asteral above. 'Tis a miracle to be surrounded by all of Zyon's friends in my midst."

Yaelas patted the monk on the shoulder. "A good friend of Zyon is a good friend of mine. What might your name be, brother?"

"Drystan," he said, peering at each of them in turn. "What prompts thee to travel through these parts? I first deemed my rescue was more by chance than anything else. Yet I sense a greater purpose for thy journey if thou have the Shadowers on thy tail."

Selest glanced at Yaelas. He nodded.

Taking a deep breath, she revealed the Key. "Our purpose is to fulfill the Quest of the Key."

The monk's eyes were the size of silver pieces. His lips fluttered open and shut but he could form no words as he observed the heavenly object.

Drystan wept quietly, a smile spreading across his face. "Doth mine eyes deceive? I've only dreamt of seeing the day." The monk closed his hands around Selest's which bore the Key. "I hope with all my heart the Quest might succeed."

She smiled. Whenever she felt alone she knew her friends were near; Asteral was near. No, He was *here*. The familiar calmness washed over her.

Chapter 21

After Drystan regained his wits, he rode on the back of Faern and directed them to the cloister. He recalled the times he and his brethren once congregated outside as he led them through the abbey. "The kitchen is just across the cloister if I remember correctly."

They rounded the corner and stopped dead in their tracks. The air smelled foul of rotting flesh. Selest gasped, eyes widened. She placed a hand over her mouth.

Rotting corpses and skeletons were gathered in piles. One had its back exposed, unveiling the torture of having its wings ripped out. The once sanctified place was now stained with the Holy Order's blood.

Carrion birds picked at the bones.

Drystan bowed his head. "Bless me. Lord forgive their transgressions. They were driven by temptation. No living mortal could've committed such a travesty. I pray one day, all once green and fair shall return to its prior state."

He turned to the others. "Come. Let us leave this place."

He led them down the hall to the servery where a long wooden slab lay upon rotting barrels.

Yaelas undid his cloak and spread it out across the floor as Thrion helped the monk down and Adair prepared to examine his wounds.

He had many infections in his arms, legs, and midsection. Adair applied sage to his open wounds. Selest wrapped them in bandages.

The monk winced as Thrion held him down, reminding Selest of her own pain.

Adair had instructed her to hold the citrus near the monk as she soothed his pain. After much struggle, Drystan's painful wheezing steadied to an even tempo as he was lulled to sleep.

Later that afternoon they had a meager lunch. As they ate, Faern spread the map out before them on the table.

He turned to Drystan. "Do you know where we're located?"

The monk shook his head. "This is a forest full of wicked deception. 'Tis impossible to know."

"Do you possess any other maps within your library?" asked Yaelas.

Selest's chest tightened. "What are we going to do?" She thought hard, racking her brain.

The monk rose. "Yes. I believe so. I can check and see what I can find—"

"Nay, lad, ye must stay seated. Let yer wounds heal."

Drystan sighed. "Very well." He turned to Yaelas. "Unless the Shadowers did away with the maps, you might findeth one."

Yaelas rose and walked past the cloister. After a long while, he returned with a handful of scrolls. He unrolled one.

"We're here nigh the northern edge of Forbid. It appears we're farther in than I anticipated."

Selest peered at the map. A monastery was drawn near a wide river, and on the western edge, a mountain range.

In the other direction, they were hemmed in by trees it seemed for miles and miles.

"How far are we from Dwindloth?" she asked.

"Sixty miles." Faern pointed at the Forbid's eastern edge. "If we're here, and continue through the forest at a swift pace, we should reach the Silver Mountains in three days' time."

"What of our provisions?"

"We've only a few days' worths o' rations left. We'll have to eat two meals daily instead of three from now on."

"And shelter?"

"There are other monasteries and huts we can camp in. It seems all evil forces have abandoned their hideouts due to war."

"How will we cross the mountain range?" asked Selest.

Adair crossed his arms. "We won't."

Selest's heart quickened. "Must we—?"

"Aye. There are mountain passages we can take beneath Dwindloth."

"It's the quickest way," said Thrion. "If we can survive Forbid, we can make it through the mines. The day of the Council continues to draw nigh."

Faern furrowed his brow and caught the wizard's eye. "Do you know the way?"

Yaelas shifted in his seat. "I've been through the northeast territory. The northwest is unknown to me."

Adair leaned back. "We'll have no trouble locating abandoned mines. That's how demons get out and about, so it's likely they're still functioning."

Dread filled the pit of Selest's stomach. Forbid? Mines? Demons?

Asteral, give me strength. She had an iron grip on the edge of the table.

Later that night, Drystan led them to a cluster of dorm rooms where they could spend the night.

The thought that these chambers once belonged to fellow monks now lying dead in the cloister sent shivers down Selest's spine. She chose a private room lined with bunks. She climbed into an upper bunk and as she peered out the window, she noticed the towering figure of Faern outside. He stood as still as a statue.

At least she was safe under the watchful eyes of her companions.

But was she safe from the fear that haunted her spirit?

Selest tossed back and forth. For the first time in a long time, she yearned to be back in her cottage in her own bed surrounded by her books. She wanted to hear the voice of her mother as she recounted many stories of fearless archangels and brave pilgrims.

Those times were gone. Every creak and crack of the ancient timbers chilled Selest to the spine. Outside, devilish cries echoed. She opened her eyes. The bottomless mines of Dwindloth gaped as a foul mouth, swallowing her whole.

Her breathing quickened. Disproportionate figures of demons towered over her.

She fell out of the upper bunk slamming the back of her head against the stone floor. She moaned in pain, rubbing the rising bump.

Someone stirred close by. A flame painted the darkness orange, illuminating the monk's gaunt face. "Dear Asteral, are you all right, child?"

She gritted her teeth. Hot tears streamed down her face. She rolled over and tried to stand to no avail. Rising to her knees, she laid her forehead on the cold stone.

She never thought she would be this relieved to be in the monastery once more. "I thought I was in the mines," she said, her breathing shallow.

"You're all right, child. It soundeth like it was just a nightmare," soothed the monk.

"I hope so." Selest rose, attempting to return to bed.

"Is there anything I can get for you?" he asked.

"Mm. I-I hit my head pretty hard—" she began as she staggered back to the ground.

"Master Dwarf!" exclaimed Drystan, rushing to her side. "I need your assistance!"

Selest felt a hand caressing her head. Shortly after, she woke to see Adair crushing an herb with his pestle. He grabbed a canteen of water and sprinkled bits into a cup from his medical bag.

"Here, it'll help calm your nerves."

Selest sipped on the water.

After a while, she noticed a peaceful warmth washing over her.

Drystan knelt beside the girl, muttering a silent prayer. She felt a cloak drape over her.

"Is she all right?" It was Thrion's voice.

"She hit the back of her head rather hard. The pain is making her go in and out of consciousness..."

Selest's vision blurred. She knew no more.

When she awoke, she noticed she was wrapped in Thrion's cloak. She felt a bandage on her head.

She looked around the cell. It was empty. Voices echoed from the hall.

Wearily, she rose. Her vision blurred and she nearly blacked out. She fetched her staff, supported her frame, and opened the door a crack as she slipped into the long hallway.

As she drew near, she discerned their voices. "...she'll have to endure." She recognized the gruff voice of Adair. "We'll have to leave her here with Brother Drystan."

"She'll be in safe hands," replied the somber voice of the monk. "Though I'd have to say it won't be safe here either. Evil still stirs in these parts, and heaven only knows where those dreadful Shadowers art as we speak."

"But she's still in no condition—," Adair countered. "Besides, she'd be safer here than traveling in the evil wastes of Fhar. The farther from that devilish door, the better."

"Only if it is what the Keybearer desires, then we shall leave her behind." The powerful voice of Yaelas silenced the dwarf. "If she believes this is her calling, don't dissuade her from it."

"If I may, Yaelas." It was the deep voice of Faern. "We can't delay any longer. The day of the Council draws nigh."

The wizard grumbled.

The color drained from her face. *Leave her here?* She extended her wings, steadying herself.

She rounded the corner. At the sight of her, everyone ceased speaking.

Selest looked at each one incredulously. "You plan to leave me here?"

Thrion approached her. "Selest—"

"I intend to fulfill this Quest." She tried to make her voice firm.

Adair furrowed his brow. "Lass, you're in no condition."

She gritted her teeth. "The enemy is marching to Orai as we speak!" she yelled, grasping her pocket as her head throbbed. "If we don't fulfill this Quest before the day of the Council, I fear what will become of the entire realm."

She stopped short. Never before had she lashed out with such ferocity. She quieted her voice. "I desire to fulfill the Quest. We've no time to waste. We ought to leave first thing this morning."

Silence.

Finally, Adair spoke. "Ye've been in and out of consciousness for two days."

"Two days?" she whispered with a white-knuckled grip on her staff.

"Aye." The dwarf looked her square in the eye. "'Tis why you shouldn't trouble yerself with such matters. Ye best get some rest an…"

"Enough!" boomed Yaelas. "We are a united company and shall remain as one. From this moment hence, no one leaves anyone behind."

Silence enveloped the room.

Thrion stepped forth. "I shall accompany you back to bed." Reluctantly, she agreed.

A deep pit of guilt gnawed at her belly as they walked along the hallway. "This is all my fault. You should've taken the Key and fulfilled the Quest without me."

"Things don't work according to *us*, but in accordance with *Him*," Thrion said. "He placed you in this very moment to fulfill His works. And you have." He looked her square in the eyes. "I know the timing may seem grim, but we are not meant to know His reasons; rather, we're to place our trust in Him. Besides," he added, "you nearly sacrificed yourself to die in my stead, and for that I owe you my life. I will ne'er leave your side. As my father said, we're a company."

Selest smiled sadly. "For that, I'm both afraid and grateful. Alas, the others don't seem to share your views."

Thrion placed a hand on her shoulder. "They only care about your safety. Yet I still deem it best that we stay together." They finally reached her door. "Adair is right about one thing."

"What?"

"You must focus on regaining your strength. The sooner you do, the sooner we can embark on the final stage of our Quest."

She peered deep into his gray eyes. "Together?"

He smiled, squeezing her shoulder. "Aye, together."

Selest patted his hand. "I'll try. Thank you for not giving up on me."

"I best go back and join the others. We have much to plan for the final stage of the journey." He withdrew. "If you need anything, you know where to find us."

Nodding, Selest shut the door behind him, retreating to her bunk.

As she lay there, she wondered if Adair and Faern were right. Perhaps it'd be best for the entire company if she stayed behind. And they had little time to spare as the day of the attack would be upon them soon enough.

She squeezed her eyes shut and prayed the forces of the Inner Realm would rally in time amid the growing darkness.

Regardless, she reminded herself that it was in Asteral's perfect timing—however hopeless it may seem. She meditated on this thought as she drifted off into a dreamless sleep.

Selest adjusted her armor before fetching her staff. Shivering, she retrieved the cloak Thrion lent her, clasping it about her before exiting the room.

A sudden burst of nervous adrenaline pushed through her veins, spurring her forward. Her heart raced as her fingers itched upon the staff.

Three days had passed when Selest was finally certain she had regained most of her strength. The company deemed it best to set off once more.

When she rounded the corner, she noticed everyone sitting at the table. Drystan was handing them provisions. "'Tis not much, but it will sustain ye for a few days of the journey."

He peered at her, his eyes cheerful despite the looming loneliness he was about to face. "Good morn, sister. 'Tis good to see thee up bright and early."

She peered thoughtfully at the monk. "Will you not accompany us, Brother Drystan?"

He sighed as the merriment in his green eyes dwindled. "Alas, I fear not. For unlike you, my spirit of adventure hath died out. Go in peace, dear one. May Asteral bear you swiftly under His wings."

As soon as he finished packing the final provisions, he handed Yaelas a map. "I believe I've provided thee with all the support I can give."

"We thank you for your generosity," said Faern with a nod.

The monk smiled. "Nay, nay. I should be thanking you. If it weren't for thy bravery I would still be locked in that cursed dungeon."

Yaelas clasped hands with the monk. "Until we meet again, brother."

Drystan said a prayer over them. "Be it in this Realm or the Eternal Sky, may Asteral keep thee and guide thee. May we all see the day that evil should pass when all rains glass."

Chapter 22

In the cold misty morning, they marched forth silently from the monastery leaving Brother Drystan behind.

Westward they went. Selest rode on Faern's back, her head still pounding from her fall.

Yaelas bore the map and led on through the cursed forest.

Selest peered through the witchcraft of Forbid, past the demonic mountains, to a land called Fhar where Tenebrose Gate lay.

They traveled past dead trees and abandoned witch camps strewn with broken cauldrons and mortal bones.

They pressed on in spite of the impending doom that grew by the moment.

They each whispered silent prayers of hope.

Selest kept thinking, *"When all rain glass, all evil may pass, all evil may pass when all rain glass."*

She thought this repeatedly for some time, as it proved to be the only source of comfort.

Sheer faith drove her onward.

As they drew closer, a desire came over her.

She grasped her pocket.

All evening they traveled until they came upon an old water mill.

They camped there that night and then continued on. The second night, they camped in an old witches' hut. For three days this cycle continued with little food and little water to spare.

Onward they trekked until the dreary mountain range loomed before them dark and merciless. With the guidance of Yaelas, the forest's magick did not hinder them.

Late in the evening of the third day they arrived. The Silver Mountain range loomed above them.

Selest's legs were like noodles as she put one in front of the other. Her stomach gnawed with hunger, and her throat felt like sandpaper.

To catch their breath, they settled near a rocky outcrop. They ate a small portion of their food and looked at the map.

"It should take us three days to travel under the mountain pass, barring any trouble," said Yaelas. "From there, another good three."

"I pray we're not too late," whispered Selest.

"It'll be close, that's for certain," said Faern. "We must be persistent. We cannot falter now. We've already lost so much precious ti—"

The sound of marching thundered in the distance.

"Quickly, over here!" Yaelas led them to a rocky wall. They all hurried around the corner, backs pressed against the stone. Nobody dared to utter a sound.

The stomping sound was in a simultaneous cadence. Selest swore her eyes deceived her, and a giant was advancing toward them. The rock beneath her feet reverberated until her bones rattled.

She seized her head as an incessant pain pounded like a hammer upon an anvil.

Bloodcurdling shrieks of demons and witches alike ripped through the air. Gradually, the clamor began to decrescendo until Selest strained to hear the faintest footsteps.

"They're taking the Border Road," said Yaelas. "Forces of Shaéél and Filiath no doubt. I deem my suspicions are confirmed: the witches and demons of Erst have sworn allegiance."

Hope bloomed in Selest's chest. "Won't they arrive late to Orai?"

Yaelas shook his head. "Not at the rate they're going."

"Witchcraft I tell ye," said Adair. "The witches' brews have increased their endurance. Alas, though rest is imperative even for the dark creatures, Yaelas is right: they show no signs of slowing down."

Thrion crossed his arms. "There's an army of at least a thousand."

Selest's heart sank.

Faern growled. "The Nephilim of Zithera are awaiting their arrival, no doubt."

Selest recalled the ambush upon the borders along the Golden Sea—only twenty miles away from the House of Orai.

That night, Selest dreaded even thinking about entering those godforsaken mines. For most of the following day, they traced the rocky outline of the mountain range until they found an opening.

Selest was wary to enter the dark passage. All she could think about was walking into the embracing claws of demons.

Not only that, but behind them, the Deceptor's army was likely already waging war against Orai.

Regardless, the land of Fhar was in their mind's eye, dawning evermore grim and terrible on the horizon. Nowhere was safe. This was the only hope they had of fulfilling the prophecy. All would go according to plan, lest ill-fortunate befell them, or worse, their own desires ambushed them.

"Is there no other way?" Selest asked as they stood at the entrance.

"The safest way is to brave the mines abandoned long ago," Yaelas told her. "If we pass by unseen by the Nephilim and witches, our only hindrance will be the uncertainty of whether demons inhabit the mines." The wizard's beard twitched as the mountains loomed over the company menacingly. He turned to Adair. "I hold little knowledge in regards to these mines. But with the map Drystan lent us, I can locate the way out. Yet are any of you familiar with the mines of the Wolvenborn?"

Adair's face was downtrodden. "Little is my knowledge concerning Dwindloth's lore, but from my sheer observation I have some small understanding of how the mines operate, though these mines may be moth-eaten from hundreds o' years o' abandonment."

"Which is all the more reason we ought to be wary," said Yaelas, peering at the grim and vast mountain range. "Foul things lurk beyond."

"But they are fighting a battle," Selest said. "They're busy fighting. Our presence should go by unnoticed, should it not?"

"Not every evil thing gets caught up with the tides of war," explained the wizard. "There is some evil that chooses to hide from the world in dark places rather than waste its time toiling in it."

Selest peered at each one of her companions, shaking her head miserably. "I don't wish for that number to grow any more than it already has."

"Faith, my young archangel," said Yaelas. "We are in good hands." His gray eyes rekindled with hope. "Take heed of Asteral's presence. Think of how far we've come."

They decided to enter the mountain passage at first light. No one could sleep that night, for dread filled their hearts as to what awaited them. Since the horses would be of no more use, they would set them loose at first light so they could find their way back home.

The next morning, they gathered what supplies they had, ate a quick breakfast, and proceeded single-file into the mine. Yaelas led the company followed by Faern, then Adair and Selest, with Thrion guarding the rear. The wizard summoned blue light from his staff to lead the way into the endless chasm, and the rest of the company carried torches lit from their campfire.

The entrance was wide enough for six dwarves to have walked through abreast, but the low, rocky ceiling proved to be a challenge.

Luckily, the door was wide enough for Selest's ten-foot wings and Faern's great stature, though they all did have to bend down.

Adair stared in awe as they journeyed into the realm of his kin.

Though Selest didn't find beauty in the barren rock, she assumed it was the riches hidden in the rock that had filled the dwarves with awe. Though it was untouched by any source of natural light, the blue radiance from the wizard's staff was just bright enough to illuminate the way for her weary eyes. Deeper, deeper the shaft descended until Selest was convinced they would suffocate in the heart of the mountain. The air grew scarce and what little air there was, was tinged with dust and decay. It reminded her of the dungeons below the monastery. But this was far worse.

"There are vents engraved in the rock," explained Adair. "That is how we get our air. But I would venture to say these vents are broken."

Their hearts sank at the dwarf's words.

Selest's grip tightened around her staff. She peered ahead at the others, leaning on her staff to support her fatigued and bent frame. What little they had eaten didn't sustain her. But she had to keep going, one foot in front of the next.

Down.
Down.
Down.

On either side of her, the rocky walls seemed to close in. She panted heavily. Then suddenly to her right and to her left darkened chasms gaped from the walls. Adair explained that these were side tunnels used to transport gems above ground. Gradually, the narrow shaft widened. The crackling flames from their torches echoed in time with the pounding of their footfalls. The sounds seemed to reverberate through chambers hidden and unseen. A glint of light caught Selest's eye. The light was so bright she mistook it for daylight—a daylight she had not seen since she entered Forbid. But as they progressed farther, she gave a gasp of awe.

The narrow passage gave way to a wide chamber full of vibrant gem light. Precious stones of aquamarine, sapphire, garnet, ruby, and diamond jutted from the gray rock. Overhead, they twinkled as a chandelier. Selest peered at a diamond the size of her foot and her reflection was mirrored in the facets. She gave a start, unsure of what she saw. Slowly she looked again. She nearly cringed at her reflection. She saw a smudged face surrounded by ratty hair. Her cheeks were hollow, and her eyes were bloodshot. Oh, how this Quest had already taken its toll on her. She peered at the others. They too were thinner and dirtier. But no less in spirit, she assured herself.

Adair's face lit up with wonder as he viewed the vast chamber filled with blue and red light. "By my beard," he whispered, "can it truly be the Treasure Trove of Faolin the First Wolvenborn?"

"Touch nothing," Yaelas warned. "We know not what traps may have been laid in this realm."

Onward the wizard led them, past the priceless gems and through another passageway. The farther they proceeded, the dimmer the gem light became. Selest's heart sank. How she missed light so pure, so beautiful. The wizard's staff illuminated a cold light that reflected runes, ancient and foreboding.

The walls rose as though to the very frame of the mountain. Halls stretched for miles and miles on end. Stone pillars expertly carved in intricate designs supported the towering arched ceiling. Selest could feel its vastness stretching out before her; the respect it demanded made her feel meek and insignificant. She squinted to discern in the very center, as far away as she could see, a darker spiral-like shape in contrast to the already grim walls.

"Where are we?" she asked, hoping Adair could answer.

"Diern Spire," replied Adair. "The very pinnacle of Dwindloth."

Selest fixed her eyes ahead where the wizard was leading them closer and closer to the tremendous spire.

She tensed as it loomed larger and larger above her. And as they passed it, behind the spectacle, she noticed a throne sitting atop a pedestal. She stopped to peer at it. "Is that the throne of Faolin?" she asked.

Adair halted. "Where?" he asked. Selest pointed east of the spire. "Can it be? By Darragh have my eyes deceived me?" he said as he approached the wonder.

"Stay!" the wizard demanded. "We do not yet know what lies yonder. This place could be crawling with demons."

"Well, if there were demons, they would have already destroyed us," said Adair.

"Tricky things they are," muttered the wizard. "I demand you not go near." He raised the staff. "I sense foul things ahead." Everyone tensed at the wizard's dire tone. After a moment or so of silence, the wizard cautiously motioned the company forward. All were relieved to be rid of that place, for it had an odd air about it. All except for Adair. He glanced back longingly at the throne as it got farther and farther from view.

As they continued to progress, it seemed miles upon miles through which they traveled, going ever deeper. Stones of dread sank into the pit of Selest's stomach. She could hardly discern how far down they were going, yet somehow she felt the weight of the ground slowly clouding her in a veil of nothingness threatening to crush her from the inside out.

She tried not to heed this feeling by counting the taps of her staff. One–two–three–no, the footfalls were too infinite. The weight of the losses the company had suffered caught up to her suddenly. Her head spun and she stumbled. She steadied herself once more with her staff.

Adair nearly tripped at Selest's abrupt halt. "Oi! Ye good?"

Thrion turned and took her arm. "Come, we're nigh whatever end awaits us, I am sure of it." With grave reluctance, Selest kept pace with Thrion's long gait. Selest felt her face burn with humiliation. Out of them all, she couldn't help but consider herself the weakest. It was a hindering thought, but regardless, all she could do was to keep pressing forward one step at a time.

After hours upon hours of endless trekking, Selest was certain she spotted a pinpoint of faint gray light in the distance. Relief flooded over her. And yet, no one else seemed to share her excitement. Then a shadow of despair loomed over her. Was it just a trick of the eye? If it was, then why was it that the closer the company got the brighter the entrance gleamed—and not as an illusion? They soon reached the mine's east entrance. Selest shielded her eyes and the gray light engulfed her as they exited the cave.

Then her heart sank. The joy she had felt was short-lived. Now, the dim ash lands of bone and tombstones of Fhar stretched out before them.

Selest turned around and gasped. For the entrance from whence they had come was no more.

Chapter 23

They were trapped in the land of Fhar. Whatever evil spell barred the mine's entrance none could tell. The only way was ever forward. Each of them looked at their companions in turn. The final chapter in their Quest had fallen upon them. The final chime of the clock that had ticked so long seemed too slow as it made the gradual, final tock. The silence was a reaper that bore a scythe to hush the living to eternal sleep. Still, they trekked on. For what else could be done? Their course was set. No words or deeds could now hinder their partaking in this Quest.

Time passed until all recollection of day or night was lost, for this was the land of neutrality. Neither sun nor moon shone upon it, and no heavenly body was visible except for the Star of Asteral. The gray soil stretched for as far as they could see. The land had such an eerie presence to it, that the companions turned to draw their weapons at any breeze or any trick of the eye.

They pressed on, eating what little rations remained.

Selest's stomach gnawed with fresh hunger, and her throat was parched until she became accustomed to the feeling.

Her vision blurred as she phased in and out of delirium.

It wasn't until they came upon a group of trees that they stopped in shock. This was the only place with any vegetation in the land of Fhar. All else was a barren wasteland compared to the sight that lay before their eyes. But as they grew closer, they found an even more peculiar sight: thousands of antique keys dangled from the trees' limbs.

In spite of her weariness, Selest gasped. Most of the keys resembled the Key of Ezelex in shape or color. The keys blew like wind chimes as a slight puff of wind whisked the company into the odd clearing. Yaelas halted before the group. Turning, he said, "Whatever you do, don't lay a finger to disturb any of the keys that hang. They are cursed by corruption."

"How did these keys come to hang here?" asked Selest.

"Each represents a failed attempt at finding the Key of Ezelex. The Deceptor ordered the Shadowers and his other agents of evil to retrieve the Key so he could destroy it so that no one could lock evil out of the Inner Realm. Many claimed to hold the Key, but many were deceived, and only wanted approval from the Devil." He bowed his head. "Your parents, my wife, and I were the first to embark on the Quest of the Key in the name of Asteral."

Selest stared at the ground. "W-was that why the Quest you embarked on failed?"

A heavy silence filled the air. Finally, Yaelas spoke, "Nay, it was because we were greatly outnumbered. In hindsight we know we did not ask for Asteral's guidance, but rather plunged ahead with our own agenda. It was not His timing. If it wasn't for Liadan's sacrifice, we would have all been dead."

"But with Deceptor's forces occupied with attacking Orai we have an advantage, right?"

"The Deceptor's forces are still great in number. It's only a matter of time before they strike us once we arrive," Thrion replied.

Selest shivered, daring a glance behind. She fixed her gaze on a looming mountain pass before her.

A spark of adrenaline mixed with dread rushed through her veins. She didn't want to die, but—they were so close, yet so far.

She could only hope that after this, the Quest would be fulfilled. Then life would return to what it once was, but never the same. She thought of this as she studied each of the keys dangling overhead. Each was made for the same purpose, to lock the Devil's gate and keep evil at bay, yet each was used for corrupted deeds.

She couldn't help but wonder; is this what she wanted? To fulfill the Quest, knowing the outcome, but yet facing the unknown as the result? She thought of the dwarves who desired to reclaim their home in the mountains; the fauns who wished to play music as wandering bards; the centaurs yearning to roam the plains free from evil hands; and the wizard and his son.

She furrowed her brow. For the duration of their journey, Yaelas and Thrion had been distant. Perhaps there was still some tension between them.

They trekked within the forest of keys, until in the distance a void blacker than night beckoned them onward, threatening to swallow them whole. Yaelas halted the company.

Turning, he said, "I don't know what will become of us, but take heed; this is where our Quest comes to an end." His face was like a gravestone. A message of regret was written upon every wrinkle. "All of you have shown true bravery by making it to the end of all ends of the world." He peered at each in turn. "I can see in your eyes the same fear that consumes half of my heart." His gaze softened with renewed hope. "Fear not, Asteral's Word is true. His timing is perfect. Whether we see life or death, the end is found in His presence."

They made the final stretch until the Devil's Gate came into view. It was unlike anything Selest imagined. The half-opened door was of the purest silver. It was also quite narrow as well and no more than eight feet high. A single keyhole was in the center. The dark opening gave way to the grayness of the land with a false sense of neutrality. Amidst the barrenness all was still. Not a single being seemed to be present.

Yaelas raised his hand signaling everyone to stop.

The wizard fixed his gaze on the girl. "I believe it is your place to close the door, but after all we have endured I will not lay this burdensome task on you if you do not wish it."

All eyes were on the young archangel. She sighed. She knew what she had to do. "My father's dying wish was for me to fulfill the Quest of the Key," she began, a lump forming in her throat, "but you were the one who entrusted this task to him and my mother long ago. So if you deem it right, I ask that I, accompanied by your son, who bore witness to my father's request to his only daughter, should see this task done."

Yaelas sighed. "If that is what you are both willing to do."

Thrion stepped forward. "If this is what is meant to be."

"I believe it is," the wizard responded.

Trembling, Selest withdrew the Key from her pocket and reached for the door. She dared not peer into the damned abyss.

A sound so faint, so unearthly, echoed from the depths. It was a sound she didn't hear but rather knew. She was overcome with a fear more tangible than the fear she felt going down the cellar to fetch the wine, or even when she entered the abyss of the dungeon to free the monk. This fear defied description.

She felt the Devil's invisible limb reach through the abyss, trying to snatch the Key.

A chill ran through her hand and deep into her heart. She jerked back and clutched the Key to her chest in shock.

"Raven!" Adair rushed to her side. A haunting scream penetrated the stillness. Selest strained to see what was happening. She caught a blinding glimpse of the faces of dark figures emerging from the deep.

Fearing for her life, Selest slammed the door and slid the Key into the lock. She struggled to turn it.

Suddenly, a heavy force caused the ground to quake. She fell back and heard a sickening *snap!*

She gasped. The Key had broken off in the lock, splitting in two down the center.

Chapter 24

All at once the sun dimmed like the waning of a candle. The gray land darkened until the entire Inner Realm was covered by the veil of night.

From the sky, starlight descended like hail. Pieces of moonlight came down as light as snow. All rained down from the gaping wounds of the heavens. Darkness was all that remained.

Selest glanced at the door. Half of the Key was there. The other half was nowhere to be seen. The door creaked open and she jumped up to try and hold it shut.

Selest wept, peering up to the heavens. "Why isn't it raining glass?" she said hysterically, examining the upper half of the Key.

So many lives were lost. They were too late. Evil won. The Devil's Gate was still open.

Asteral, if you are there, give me eyes to find what I seek. Evil didn't want the Key to fulfill its Quest. That is what they had to fight against. *Asteral, give me eyes to see.*

In the Eternal Book, the prophecy was written; she believed it to be true. *Give me eyes to see.* All will rain pure. For a better end. She kept reminding herself.

She found herself on the edge of the story, waiting to obey what she and her friends were called to do. They were characters in a tale bigger than themselves. *Asteral you are my eyes.* From the darkness Selest was, and she will be. *Asteral, you are the Key.*

"Raven!"

"Selest!"

Her friends rushed to her aid, helping her bar the door.

"I failed," she sobbed. "I failed us all."

A mighty roar of demons and other unnamed evil creatures reverberated in her chest, as they charged out of nowhere from behind her.

Selest looked on in terror as the army of wicked forces attacked the company within the darkness.

Yaelas stood before the agents of evil and summoned a ball of white light, blinding the enemy's minions. She knew he was buying them time. Faern and Adair pressed hard against the door with all of their might, trying to keep it sealed.

The five companions found themselves trapped with evil on either side of them. But no matter their strength, the door creaked open bit by bit.

Selest saw the arm of a creature with eyes blacker than death. The same limb reached out, trying to snatch the Key from its lock.

She screamed. The Devil's hand touched the Key, only to recoil. The Devil let out a bone-chilling cry that shook the entire Inner Realm.

All at once the door burst open, letting all Hell break loose. The same limb reached for the other half of the Key which Selest had retrieved and held firmly in her hand. She closed her eyes. Awaiting the final blow, her entire body trembled.

As she dared to peek at the horror before her a flash of gray passed through her line of vision, followed by a sickening *thud!*

"No!" she gasped.

Thrion stood before her, his chest bleeding heavily.

"The prophecy...is fulfilled."

She froze. "No—I failed."

"The prophecy has always been fulfilled—Asteral has always been the Key—" Blood poured from his mouth. Thrion's eyes dimmed. "Now, go... fulfill this Quest..."

With the last of his strength, Thrion shielded her body with his, warding off any demon in her path with his bare hands.

At that moment, an assembly of angels leading chariots of fire drawn by white steeds descended from the heavens. They wielded swords forged of heavenly silver as they met the Deceptor's agents of evil in battle. As they clashed, glass rained from the heavens, piercing only the enemy and depleting their ranks.

Her companions gave a war cry. With renewed hope they charged into the melee.

But Selest remained behind, knowing what she had to do. She picked up her staff. Turning, she faced the Devil, the Key clenched in her hand.

The onslaught between demons and Asteral's creation slowed around her. Her hand holding the upper fragment of the Key trembled.

Without warning, the Devil leaped after her.

Selest spread her wings and soared into midair amidst the glass that fell from the sky. She held up the broken half of the Key, and it began to shine on its own accord growing brighter and brighter as Selest ascended.

Then she looked down upon the horrid scene. The demons shielded their eyes as the light of the Key blinded them.

She glanced at the rest of her companions. She descended to meet her foe, piercing him with the Staff of Crysil. The Devil gave a blood-curdling shriek as he fell.

Selest landed upon the corpse-strewn ground. She raised her staff triumphantly.

"The battle has already been won!" she declared. A heavenly light encircled Selestial, as she held the Key in hand.

Then all at once, a mighty gale from the heavens sucked the Devil and his army into the Abyss. The door slammed closed with a mighty *thud*!

As it did, Selest noticed the lower fragment of the Key was still inserted in the lock. She dropped her staff and ran to the door. With both hands, she seized the key and tried to turn it with all her weight. The jagged crystal bit deep into her flesh.

She screamed in pain as a bitter cold seeped into her hands. But still, she turned with all her might. Finally, she heard a faint *click*! All at once, the door fastened shut with an unnatural force.

Suddenly, the glass rain that had helped conquer their enemies turned to water and then stopped altogether. The host from Heaven retreated. The dark and barren sky was filled with starlight.

As they peered up at the darkness, they beheld the star, Asteral's Remnant, shining brighter than any light that had ever shown within the Inner Realm.

Selest gasped, for the three-pointed star had become a two-pointed star.

The prophecy was fulfilled.

Chapter 25

As suddenly as it had happened, the war between the heavenly host and the Devil's advocates ceased. Selest seized the two broken pieces of the Key in either hand and knelt before her savior.

"Thrion!" she cried. She winced from the pain of her hand. The blood drained from her face. Thrion lay there, paralyzed on the corpse-strewn ground. Sweat drenched his face as he panted heavily. "Thrion, I'm here."

Thrion peered up at the starry sky. She followed his gaze. She was almost certain the host of angels would peek from the empty veil once more, for she could feel their presence. It was an endearing thought, but at the same time she marveled at the idea of an entire triad peering down upon them— mere archangels of the lowest triad.

"It's over," she whispered, turning to face Thrion. "It's done."

Thrion withdrew his necklace, handing it to her as his eyes focused beyond her. "Ah, Selestial, it's so beautiful."

Selest grasped his hand holding the necklace. "What do you see?" she asked.

"I see…" Thrion took his final breath. His hand went limp in her grip.

She sat there, floating between the clouds of angelic tranquility and the chasm of the Abyss. The vast expanse was an ocean of cold peace calling her home. The heaviness of reality set in.

The company gathered around the hunter's body, withdrawing their weapons and paying homage to their fallen comrade.

The wizard knelt beside his son. Yaelas bowed his head, sobs wracking his body. "Ah, my son, first your mother and now you, all because of trying to fulfill the Quest." He knelt beside his corpse. "May Asteral welcome you with open arms."

They took his body across the land of Fhar and passed through the Tenebrose Gate, burying him in the Misty Forest. They made camp there, in the very cottage where the Silverans had lived as a family.

The darkness of night cloaked them and Selest shivered as a blanket of dampness settled on her chest.

A slight throb pained her hand while her eyes adjusted to the darkness. As Adair bandaged her hand, she reminisced of the Quest and all that had taken place.

Selest peered out the window at the stars peeking out from the trees' silhouetted limbs. There, Asteral's Remnant shone brightest. The faint blue glow of Yaelas' staff radiated throughout the darkness. The light engulfed the companions as he made a fire in the old fireplace.

Faern approached, withdrawing an assortment of nuts and berries he collected from the Misty Forest.

He handed Selest a handful. "Here. 'Tis not much, but it'll do."

She felt the gnawing in the pit of her belly. "Thank you, Faern," she whispered. Through tears, she looked out the window and saw Yaelas sitting beside the freshly dug grave.

A lump caught in her throat. "Oh, Faern."

The centaur wrapped his arms around her, stroking her wings. Silent tears rolled down the centaur's eyes. Adair sat beside them, staring at the flames.

From where they sat, they heard Yaelas weeping. "Ah, my son. You were on the verge of manhood, and already you had accomplished so much. You and your mother achieved what I could not. You gave your lives for the good of this Quest." He choked. "I hope that one day I may see the good in its fulfillment as well. You and your mother are at peace now, free from the evils of this world."

That night, Yaelas did not eat or drink. He only wept in the darkness. He wept until the rising sun exposed his most vulnerable self once more to the dawn of a New Era.

The next morning, they traveled south on the road toward The Glade. The smell of rotting decay stung Selest's eyes and nose. She nearly gagged.

That was when they realized the terrible truth. The corpses of dwarves, centaurs, and fauns mixed with the corpses of witches and demons alike littered the way.

Faern guessed as soon as the enemy learned of their intentions, they retreated toward Fhar—only to be stopped by the forces of opposition. It was hard to say who the victor would have been had the prophecy not been fulfilled.

When they finally reached The Glade, they continued until Selest stumbled upon a familiar sight. Her heart stopped. It was her home, the one she left behind all those months ago.

"So this is what is left of the House of Inriser," spoke the voice of Yaelas.

She said nothing. Without another word, she walked past the lawn and onto the threshold. She turned to her companions.

Their eyes peered at her. No words were spoken as Selest slowly pivoted and walked past the broken door, past the dining area, and into the hallway.

She gasped, covering her gaze. There, she stopped short. For there lay the bones of her father; carrion birds and vermin had picked his bones clean. She collapsed beside the grevious sight.

The wizard knelt beside her. "I'm deeply sorry for what befell your dear father."

Select nodded. "Thank you. Though if it weren't for you all those years ago the Key wouldn't have come to my father or me. I know it was wrong of him to hide it from me after my mother told him to fulfill her dying wish, but I think things have a way of conforming to Asteral's will."

"All for the better," added Yaelas. "I know it is hard to see things in such a way, but your father's mistakes were the doorway of opportunity for you, my young owl-wing." He placed a hand on her shoulder. "Now that the prophecy has been fulfilled, a new era has unfolded."

She withdrew the broken Key. "I fulfilled the Quest, Father," she whispered. "It is done."

Sighing, she peered at her companions in turn.

"I have a favor to ask of all of you," she said. "You are right, Yaelas, that I will find rest in my heart as I mourn for my father. Would all of you please help me bury him?" She quickly added, "I know 'tis unfair of me to ask, when some of your kin lay at rest as well, with no burial site to tend to."

"After what you have achieved in this Quest, your favor would be an honor to fulfill," spoke Faern. "Your compassionate character alone is what I respect the most, and as a token of my appreciation, I will gladly help in laying your father to rest."

Select's face broke into a smile. "Thank you."

"I would like to help as well, Raven," Adair said. "It's the least I can do."

Adair fashioned a makeshift stretcher, and Faern and Yaelas settled the body of Savion Inriser upon it.

Select led them to the family grave. The silent procession made its way to the clearing. She wished for her father to be buried beside her mother.

The dwarf dug a grave beside Select's mother. When that was done, they placed her father in the grave.

Select sprinkled white blossoms from the tree above onto her father's body before Adair shoveled patches of dirt into his grave.

On the gravestone, Faern carved the name Savion. When this was all completed, Yaelas said a short prayer.

As they returned to the cottage and went up the porch steps, Select gasped at the splintered door covered in blood. She clenched her stomach with her uninjured hand.

"Ye don't have to if ye don't want to just yet, lass," Adair reassured her.

"I–I need to see my mother," she rasped.

Select entered the house and walked past the splintered door and debris. Select peered down the hallway to where the portrait of her mother hung.

It was still intact, though rather faded. She gazed at the archangel's light skin with her blue eyes and crow-black hair.

She walked over and placed a hand on the painted face.

Turning, she went upstairs to her room, and Adair followed. As she entered, she noticed everything was in disarray. All was deathly quiet.

Parchment and books littered the floor. She noticed a book with the cover open. The title page read: *The Song of Elarael*. She picked it up, turned to the first page, and recited the poem aloud to Adair:

In days of old, it was foretold,
Of a young Angelic Maiden
Foreshadowed to be ladened
Whose name echoed the stars;
Pure light is seen from afar.
Elarael! Elarael!
A Pure Seraph on high,
In the ever-darkening blacklight,
Her wings were glimmering white;
A beacon in the sky.
Her hair was as raven as the night.
And her eyes of starlight never ceased.
For she possessed the gift of foresight
And was known as HighSeer of the East.
But soon, forever to be deprived of her might.

'Twas the eve of night,
The moon shone forever fair and bright,
And the stars were all alight.
Casting down a heavenly crown,
Mirroring the divinity of the Seer.
Freer of the dark,
In which the stars gleam but a spark.
Guiding those to the light they seek,
On the edge of night the very peak.
Shimmering white water flowing.
The wind, evermore blowing.
Down nigh the glade mere,
Her spirit shall appear.
Ascending on forevermore,
O'er the Crystal Shore.

The Witches of Shaeel beheld her splendor;
And hark! The mighty herald fell.
For the dagger forged of Embrethel made its mark,
Her wings were cut down to the root.
As she tried to flee in cold pursuit.
Elarael the Fallen,
In this name, she shall dwell.
The blade ran cold with angelic blood,
The blood of her kin.
As the pain burned the flames of Hell,
So did her pride within.
They left on the brink of twilight,
Nothing but a phantom in the dawning light.
For behold, there lay the wingless maid!
A loner in the shadowy glade.
She wandered the forest o'er,
Within the realm along the shore.
She stopped and looked along the moor,
And saw her Sister Star there shimmering;
The star of Angli in all its glory glimmering.
'Twas a bright lantern shining in the deep,
She traveled o'er the silvery path it bore,
Till she beheld a mighty keep.
Etched in the silver lining of the shore,
Before her lay the mystic earth,
The whitening light of rebirth.

Through eyes of wonder, she beheld,
The glowing aura on the endless fell.
Piercing the depths of the abyss,
Spellbound with eternal bliss.
She stood upon stars dancing,
One with Eternity without glancing.
In her spirit glimmering,
On the verge of divine shimmering.
Lo and behold!
She was a beacon in the night once more,
Just as it was foretold in days of old.
Elarael the Fallen has been Reborn!
And shalt be Forevermore!

Archangel of the Heavens,
Diviner of the Crystal Shore!

Adair smiled. "She reminds me of you, Raven."

Selest returned the smile.

Carrying the book, she and the dwarf descended the stairs and exited the house.

They both hastened north across the clearing, approaching the Inriser family headstone.

Chapter 26

Sinking to her knees before the engraved granite, the day slowly closed its gray curtain about her. She sighed as she laid her book down before the freshly dug grave. She covered her face with her wings, shielding her from the same cold breeze that rustled the leaves. Shivering, she rested her eyes on the book's worn, blue cover. With a shaking hand, she lifted the cover and turned to the opening page. The faded ink on the stained yellow parchment read, *To my dearest daughter, Selestial, may your thoughts and prayers always heed His wisdom.*

It was three years ago on Starry Eve when her life was changed forever. She peered above as the evening settled upon the gloom of the earth. Hugging her loved ones' headstone, she whispered into the granite, "It is done, mother, it is done, your dying request has been fulfilled." She rested her head on the monument and closed her eyes.

She awoke as footsteps approached.

Yaelas knelt beside her as their other companions gathered around. "We've decided to camp here and part ways early in the morning."

Selest gave a start at this news but said nothing. Why should she be surprised? The Quest was over, so of course the company would disband. They had their homes to go to, did they not? She sighed at the idea of life without her friends.

Yaelas' gaze fell to the Lone Road a few feet away from where they sat. "My son was very fond of you. He admired your courage. He said it was because of you that his faith in Asteral strengthened."

She was startled. "Me?"

"It was your sacrifice."

Selest also peered at the Lone Road. "It seems like forever ago. Thrion was riding down the road in this direction." She forced a laugh. "I mistook him for a Shadower at first."

Yaelas chuckled. "You've had many strange folks come to your home."

Selest stole a glance in his direction. It did seem like a lifetime ago that the Quest began. "Where are you going to go?" she asked. "Will you return to the Misty Forest?"

Yaelas shifted uneasily. "I plan to travel to Snowtown to aid Brother Zyon and Brother Drystan in rebuilding the Church."

She smiled. "Tell them I said hello, and—" Her heart sank. "What of the rest of you?"

The centaur sighed. "I plan to resettle the land of Perisade and return it to its former glory."

"Aye. I wish to see that for the Silver Mountains as well." Adair crossed his arms. "Granted, it'll take time, but it is the start of a new Era." Adair turned to Selest. "What of you, Raven?"

She faced her house. "My heart still belongs here. I want to fix up our farm and make a library where I can read, and have a desk where I can write about my adventures. And yet," her voice faltered, "a part of me wants to be with you all. How do I know what to do?"

Yaelas rose. "Pray to Asteral to give you guidance; it would be more wisdom than I could ever give."

She nodded, retrieving her book. "Let's go to the porch and talk for a time, like old friends, before you're on your way."

With that, they turned and went back to the house. The company settled in under the night sky. In spite of trying to be strong, she peered at the doorway in grieving earnestness.

She lowered her head.

"Cheer up," Yaelas said soothingly. "The witches are conquered, and now you may find rest in your heart as you can finally grieve the loss of your father in peace. As for tonight, we shall remember together, recalling all that has taken place as we too grieve for those slain."

The stars gleamed brightly, and then brighter still. To everyone's amazement, faes of sapphire, gold, silver, and emerald appeared to grace the night. For after the prophecy was fulfilled, and when it rained glass all those days ago, word had spread that the evil forces of the world were once again imprisoned.

Many creatures of the Enchanted Forest and beyond the westward horizon migrated back to the West to enchant those grayed lands again. It so happened that despite the splendor of the faes the company had witnessed back in the Enchanted Forest, they were delighted once more with an ever brighter display than before. For it was as though the stars had descended from Heaven to grace the dead world below. All was fair and memorable that night.

The company made camp beside Savion's grave. There they mourned and recalled past tidings before the Quest, before the Siege of the West, and before rumors of war had reached their minds.

They recalled mining for gems as pure as starlight, frolicking in fields once lush and green, making music with the chime of the wind, sitting peacefully underneath the ancient oaks, and hearing the ever-slight voice of their tales. They shared all these memories bright in truth, with souls intertwined in the faeries' radiant hues which reflected the hearts of the now dyadic stars.

Shadows advanced. Everyone tensed. "Who goes there?" asked Faern.

They drew their weapons as the shadows grew closer.

Selest's heart caught in her throat. She discerned gray shapes of a faun, a man, a stooped winged being, and a slender centauress.

"It can't be," she whispered.

Warily, she approached the road. "D-Drystan? Etris?"

The foremost figure withdrew his hood, revealing a pair of solemn green eyes.

Selest embraced the monk. "How'd you all come here?"

Etris replied, "A messenger came to my doorstep and told me of an evil scheme to destroy all the leaders of the Inner Realm. A group of my faes and I journeyed to Orai where many were gathered in preparation for battle."

Oskar nodded. "I overheard Etris saying you passed by her parts. I told her I journeyed with you from the White Owl Inn."

"I couldn't help but overhear as well," Astria blushed. "We escaped the worst of the battle and have been searching for survivors ever since."

Faern approached Astria, his brows furrowed. "How do you fare?"

She lowered her head. "Not many survived. Many forces arrived as soon as they could, but we were overwhelmed."

Selest sighed. "We were too late in fulfilling the Quest. If we would've fulfilled it sooner—"

Etris raised her lantern. "The Quest is fulfilled, child. Many hath tried but their efforts came to naught. One truly ponders Asteral's timing and questions why. And He answers—Be still, and know I Am."

"This world is just a fleeting thing." Yaelas peered at the stars above. "This isn't our home. Ours is in the Eternal Sky. And I know my son is watching down o'er us all."

Astria lifted her head as well. "So is Adhearn. He was as a father to me."

Selest raised her gaze, peering beyond the hedge, beyond the endless sky, and fathomed the bright celestial gates. There, she envisioned Thrion and her family observing her in this temporary realm. And though a vast chasm lay between them, she felt her loved ones right next to her, closer than ever.

She and Drystan would remain behind, and with the help of the faes they would restore what was lost in Sovoria.

Early the next morning, when the dew was crisp upon the leaves of trees and blades of grass, the company prepared to depart. Selest tried to hold back tears while she observed the company packing their essentials for the journey east. Drystan approached her, his eyes sparkling with a joy that could only be found through the Spirit of Asteral. His expression wavered when he saw the young maiden's pensive face. "I take this parting as a sorrowful moment."

She lowered her head. "After all the trials we have endured together, why must we depart from each other's company? It only seems right if we remain as one and face the good and the bad together."

The friar stood there for a moment in earnest pondering. Finally, he spoke: "Asteral has many plans in store. Sometimes, these plans lead us down different paths. But if we continue to walk in agreement with Him, in the end, we shall all travel that same narrow road. But for now," he turned to face Selest tenderly, "this goodbye is only temporary."

She forced a smile. "It is temporary, yes, but that doesn't mean the parting won't be hard."

"Have faith, child. Today is a new day and someday, in your lifetime, we shall all meet again." With that prophetic word, Selest's faith grew a little bit stronger.

The others vowed to do the same throughout the Inner Realm.

After a few moments, Adair, Faern, and Yaelas were ready to set off.

Reluctantly, Selest approached them on the edge of the Lone Road. They all stood in a straight line, with faces grim, though Selest could see right through their stone-like facades.

She stood before them gazing at each with longing eyes and thanked Asteral for the beautiful relationships she would always treasure.

"You have been with me through it all," she said. "I cannot fathom this to be the end."

She gave a brief pause of silence. "When the Key came to me, my family and home were stripped away, yet I had hope in my heart to fulfill my parents' dying wish and to return home." Her voice began to waver, as she stretched out her hands. "And I did. But now I realize I am not home. My home is being stripped away from me once more." A heavy silence ensued. "You are all my home," she whispered, "and no measure is strong enough to unravel the strings of love that bind us. But my heart still aches at the thought of saying goodbye."

The company broke into tears at the young girl's words. "If any of you ever stop by, or if we ever have a chance meeting, I-I will always be open to converse about adventures, gold, theology, anything." Her face broke into a smile.

With one final glance, she turned away. Selest trod the dry grass until her gaze rested on her family's grave site. Silent tears streamed down her face.

Whether the tears were from a place of sorrow or joy she did not know. It was perhaps both. She placed a hand upon her face and stood still as she sobbed. Her wings drooped behind her, sheltering her from the farewell scene, and she pressed her hand against the blue star Thrion had borne.

"Asteral, be near me," she prayed. "Are You still there?" At that moment, a cold breeze whipped about her, like an embrace, wiping away her tears.

I am here, Selestial. Always.

She felt light, as though she was awakened in a sweet dream. She opened her eyes to see if she was truly in a dream.

Epilogue

Wandering upon the Lone Road, an old dwarf merchant traveling in an expedition from the Silver Mountains stopped in his tracks. A tombstone caught his attention.

He knelt beside the gravestone, tracing the etchings. On the bottom was a glass case where the Key of legends was laid to rest.

He stopped short. "By my beard. It seems ages ago. Aye." He placed a hand gently on the glass, remembering.

The sound of hoof falls startled the grayed dwarf.

"Hail, lonely merchant."

He turned and was greeted by five centaurs. "Well, if it isn't Faern the Fearless if I do rightly recall."

The old centaur grinned. "'Tis good to see an old friend. It's been too long."

"Aye." He glanced past him to a familiar centauress and the three young centaurs standing regally beside their parents.

They stood as though their war leader was before them, and would follow him loyally to battle. "You have raised your sons well, Faern. I see a fire in their eyes kindled in the likeness of their father."

Faern bowed his head in humble earnestness. But the dwarf noticed a spark of pride in the veteran's twinkling eyes. "Come, we best not keep our host waiting."

As they crossed the clearing, the dwarf held back a bit, observing the homestead.

He noticed that in spite of the Siege of the West, the house had been restored to its former glory. The interior was lit by golden light.

He squinted at the scene framed in the window, spying a slender figure with a pale face crowned with blue-gray hair.

He saw a monk reciting a prayer before a hanging mantelpiece of a star, and an old fawn strumming his lyre.

"Pray, are you coming?" asked the centaur.

The old dwarf was startled by his thoughts. "Yes, one moment." He turned, withdrawing a crow feather, and placed it before the grave. Turning, he caught up with the others.

As they drew closer, he caught the sound of a familiar tune sung on such occasions.

As he approached the threshold, the door opened.

A flood of yellow light cascaded around the woman, creating an ethereal glow. Her bright gray hair was unbound, falling about her thin frame. Her wings were still the same white arches of light that he remembered.

"Hello, Raven."

Pronunciation Guide

Places

Alrisite	Al-reh-site
Ban Ur	Ban Er
Brandemere	Brand-eh-mere
Cair Gaoth	Car Gae-ath
Emen Marshes	Eh-men
Everea	Eh-ver-uh
Fallendell	Fah-lin-dell
Fhar	Far
Fields of Shile (Silence)	Shile
Fionn (Black Icelands)	Fie-on
Galielle	Gal-ee-el
Glascia	Glae-she-a
Gorm Buaic	Bwae-ic
Miriand	Meer-ee-and
Municua	Mu-ni-sooa
Orai	Or-aye
Perisade (Emerald Dells)	Pear-eh-sade
Pharis Sea	F-air-is
Shaeel	Shah-eel
Shadenfell	Shay-den-fell
Tenebrose Gate	Ten-eh-brose
Tharofen	Thair-oh-fen
White Mountains (Carahadrim)	Cair-uh-ha-drim
Zithera	Zi-ther-a

Characters

Aiden	Ae-den
Adair	Uh-dehr
Adhearn	Ad-hern
Alessenger	Uh-less-in-jer
Asteral	A-ster-ul
Arasiel	Uh-raa-zay-el
Astria	As-tree-a
Caz	
Celtan	Cel-tan
Conan	K-oh-n-uh-n
Crysil	Cri-seel
Darragh	Dar-ah
Drystan	Dri-sten
Elarael	Eh-lahr-ae-el
Etris	Eh-tris
Faeodan	Fae-oh-dun
Faern	Fae-ern

Garren	Gar-ren
Ixilion	Ix-il-ee-on
Líadan	Lee-uh-den
Orla	Or-lah
Oskari	Ah-scar-ee
Quil the Deceptor	
Rofur	Roe-fer
Savion	Say-vee-un
Selestial	Suh-les-tee-ul
Thrion Silveran	Thr-aye-un
Yaelas Silveran	Yale-as
Zyon	Z-aye-on

Other

Anglï	Aang-glee-aye
Diern Spire	Dye-ern
Evenmint	Eh-vyn
Ezelex	Eh-zeh-lex
Emberthel	Em-ber-thel
Sovoria (Race of Archangels)	Soe-vor-ee-ah
Xithe	Xith

Acknowledgments

I would like to thank everyone who helped me along this amazing journey. It's been three incredible years since I started this journey. And I can't believe I've made it.

First, I would like to thank Ann Stolfa for putting in countless hours of editing my second draft. Thank you so much for taking the time and effort to share this journey with me.

Second, I would like to thank Laura Paulas and Shelley Plett from Hillsboro Free Press for helping me with the formatting, cover design, copyrighting, and production of my book. If I hadn't gotten an internship there, I would never have made the connections to make this all happen.

Third, I would like to thank Traci Matt for taking the time and effort to edit my book and making it sound ten times better than before!

Fourth, thank you so much Mom and Dad for always putting up with my endless banter about this special project of mine. Especially Mom, for being my BETA reader and putting in the time to critique my book."

Thank you, Mark Jost, for reading my painful first draft and answering all of my questions. You made me see the reality of being a writer. I would never have been the ruthless word-cutter I am if it wasn't for you.

Thank you to the rest of my friends and family (you know who you are). Thank you for your many suggestions and critiques along the way. This book would never have gotten to this point if it wasn't for your wonderful support and much-needed advice.

A huge thank you to David Loewen for taking the time and effort to improve my map of the Inner Realm. You've made this world come to life in so many ways.

And finally, I want to thank the One who made this all possible. Thank you, God, for believing in me when no one else did. When I was in my darkest moment as well as my brightest, you were there guiding me every step of the way. I couldn't have done it without You.

www.ingramcontent.com/pod-product-compliance
Lightning Source LLC
Chambersburg PA
CBHW030506260626
47157CB00005B/1682